Clara and the Cowboy

Erica Vetsch

Heartsong Presents

In memory of Lorraine Elizabeth Vetsch.
I miss you.

A note from the Author:
I love to hear from my readers! You may correspond with me by writing:

Erica Vetsch
Author Relations
PO Box 721
Uhrichsville, OH 44683

ISBN 978-1-60260-770-5

CLARA AND THE COWBOY

All scripture quotations are taken from the King James Version of the Bible.

All of the characters and events in this book are fictitious. Any resemblance to actual persons, living or dead, or to actual events is purely coincidental.

Our mission is to publish and distribute inspirational products offering exceptional value and biblical encouragement to the masses.

PRINTED IN THE U.S.A.

one

Idaho Territory, 1883

A bullet shattered the window frame beside Clara Bainbridge's cheek, and in an instant drowsiness fled. Robbers! She gritted her teeth, heart thumping.

Another shot ricocheted off the door. The driver cracked his whip, shouting at the six-horse team. The coach lurched like a drunken cowboy.

Clara tumbled to the floor amid the packages and parcels that had shared her seat. She hit her chin on a fellow traveling companion's knee, rattling her teeth and sending a jolt through the top of her head.

"Wha—?" The passenger—*Sparks, ma'am, call me Sparks*—rocketed upright, blasted from his nap by the commotion. He blinked, floundering. "What's going on?"

Clara scrabbled and swayed, trying to find a good purchase to propel herself upright again. Her pulse threatened to jump out of her throat. More gunshots sounded, some thudding into the coach, others whining past overhead. Sparks's flailing elbow dislodged her hat and sent her carefully pinned hair tumbling into her eyes. Sprawled as she was in the minimal floor space, she could hardly tell up from down. Her hand found the edge of the bench, and she dragged herself onto the seat once more.

"The floor might be a safer place for you, Miss Bainbridge." Mr. Devers, the other man in the coach, raised his voice to be heard above the clamor. Polished, polite, and devilishly handsome, he seemed none too worried over their present situation. The poor greenhorn had no idea the peril they were in. He and Mr. Sparks had boarded the stage in Elko and appeared to be traveling together. Though truthfully, Clara hadn't paid too much attention to the pair. She had focused all her attention on how close she was to home. And seeing *him* again.

Of course, all that had changed when the first bullet hit the stage.

"How many are there?" Sparks tried to stick his head through the window but yanked back when a bullet chipped the paint near his ear. He drew his pistol and checked the chambers.

Mr. Devers stuck his head out then pulled back in, blinking hard. "It's so dusty I can't tell. Several, I should think."

Clara braced herself in the corner, gripping the window frame and the edge of the seat. The coach hit a rock or gully and bounced into the air. The horses' hooves thundered on the dry ground, harnesses jingling, wheels clattering. The weaving motion grew so wild Clara feared the coach would somersault over at any moment. The acrid smell of gunpowder pinched her nose.

"Hyah! Get up! Hyah!" the driver urged the team, his whip popping like bacon on a hot skillet. The coach careened on its springs. A heavy boom sounded overhead. The messenger must've applied his shotgun to the situation.

"We'll never outrun them." Sparks craned his neck, trying to see without getting his head shot at. "We're coming to a steep grade. Wish my rifle wasn't in my pack on the roof."

Clara closed her eyes against the whirling landscape and sent up a prayer. *Lord, we need some help here. Anything You'd care to do to intervene would be much appreciated.*

At that moment, the driver screamed.

Clara's eyes flew open just in time to see his body drop past the window and tumble into the dirt. She gulped and blinked. *That wasn't exactly what I meant, Lord.*

Before anyone could react, masked thieves surrounded the slowing coach.

Clara dared a peek out the window toward the team. A man grabbed the bridle of the near leader and dragged his head around, slowing the team to a halt. The resulting silence rang in Clara's ears, and anxiety skittered up her arms. She groped for her reticule, finally finding it on the floor.

"All right. I want you to toss any guns on the ground and come out with your hands up." The voice came from Mr. Devers's side of the coach. "And you up there, throw down that scattergun and climb down real slow."

Clara looked at Mr. Devers. His thin moustache twitched, his lips pressing into a straight line. Sparks shifted the plug of tobacco in his cheek and shrugged. With a flip, his revolver sailed through the window and landed on the ground with a thud.

"Now the rest of them."

Four men, or more? Long tan dusters, hats pulled down, each with a bandana hiding the lower part of his face. Their horses, shaggy and blowing after the chase, held their heads low, lathered sides heaving. Saddle tramps, hard men.

Clara tried to wet her lips, but her mouth was too dry.

The messenger's form passed the window, his dirty boots stopping momentarily on the wheel before lowering onto the road. He lifted his hands and laced his fingers on top of his hat.

Mr. Devers brushed his coat and adjusted his cuffs. "That's all the guns. We're coming out." He reached through the window of the door and found the handle.

"Nice and slow. And keep those hands up. I've got a hair

trigger and a jumpy finger."

Sparks and Devers climbed down first.

Clara picked up her reticule and looped the strings around her wrist. She shoved her disheveled hair away from her face, dislodging a couple of hairpins in the process. With trembling hands, she grasped the door frame and scooted into the opening.

Mr. Devers put his hands on her waist and lifted her from the coach. When she stood in the rock-strewn road, he stepped in front of her, putting himself between her and the robbers. "Gentlemen, to what do we owe the pleasure?" His cultured voice sounded strange amongst the sagebrush, junipers, and lawbreakers surrounding them.

"Stand still with your hands up and keep your tater traps shut." The leader rested his wrist against his saddle horn, an action that put his pistol at eye level to Mr. Devers.

Mr. Devers raised his hands.

Clara peeked over his shoulder. Her heart thudded in her ears. *Lord, don't let them do something stupid. Just let them take what they came for and leave us alone.*

Sparks, hands up as bidden, kept his eyes on the pistol. He spat a long stream of tobacco juice into the bushes beside the road but said nothing.

One of the robbers climbed atop the stage and rummaged through the baggage.

Clara frowned when he tossed her valise to the ground. If he'd broken anything in there, she'd blister him.

"They bolted the box down."

"Well then, empty it up there." The leader rolled his eyes. "Dumb as a turnip."

"That box is the property of the Elko-Money Creek Stage Line. You break into it, they'll hang you." The messenger stood tall, his eyes cold pinpoints. His handlebar moustache obscured his upper lip. Clara could almost see the waves of frustration flowing from him. As the stage messenger, his sole job was to prevent anyone from taking the contents of the lockbox.

"They'll have to catch us first. Shoot that lock and be quick about it."

Clara jerked as two quick shots shattered the morning air. The man up on the stage lifted a handful of paper-wrapped notes and a bag that jingled with the sound of coins.

"See, just like the boss said. Miners' payrolls for Silver City and Money Creek." The leader's dark eyes glittered above his bandana. "Get it in the saddlebags, and let's get out of here."

"What about them?" The man beside the box waved a handful of money toward the passengers. "They probably have some valuables on them."

"Search them quick then. We ain't got time to lollygag around here."

One of the robbers swung off his shaggy pinto and sauntered over and shoved Mr. Devers. "Line up here, and quit hiding that gal."

Mr. Devers stepped to Clara's right, putting her between himself and Sparks, next to the coach. The bandit shoved his pistol into Devers's midsection. "Wallet and watch."

For a long moment, Devers stared down his aristocratic nose at the outlaw.

"Please, Mr. Devers. Just give them what they want," Clara whispered up at him. "Don't push them too far."

He frowned. Long, tapered, well-kept fingers reached into his jacket and withdrew a wallet.

The robber snatched it, then grabbed at the watch chain and yanked, ripping Mr. Devers's vest pocket off.

Sparks spit again. "I ain't got nothin' but my poke." He tugged a pouch from his hip pocket.

The outlaw grabbed it and tossed it in the air a few inches, a satisfied smirk around his eyes at the metallic clink. The robber turned his attention to Clara. "What you got in that purse, lady?"

The smell of sweaty horse and unwashed outlaw surrounded her. She wanted to gag. With chilly fingers, she clutched her bag. "Nothing that would be of interest to you."

The leader scanned the horizon. "Time to go, Hack."

"Ain't we got time for a little sport? That gal's a looker. I say we take her along." The man called Hack shifted the wad of tobacco in his cheek, exposing his stained teeth and lips.

Clara gasped. "If you so much as lay a hand on me, I'll—" She raised her fist to fight him off if necessary, but her action was cut off.

Mr. Devers held her wrist, pushing it down and behind him, easing himself in front of her again. "Leave her alone. Miss Bainbridge is a lady, not some dance-hall trollop. If you try to touch her, you'll have me to deal with." Not the brightest thing to say considering he was facing armed men.

The runty fellow swung his gun up and smashed Mr. Devers in the jaw.

Mr. Devers's head rocked back, striking the side of the coach. He staggered against Clara. She grappled with his weight, helping him upright once more. Blood oozed from the corner of his mouth.

Hard hands clamped onto Clara's forearm. "Come with me, pretty gal. We kin have some fun." The outlaw's eyes glittered.

Anger surged through her. She swung at him with her free hand, glad when her open palm collided with the man's cheek. He howled and reeled back, but didn't let go of Clara's arm, dragging her with him as he stumbled.

The leader lifted his reins and urged his horse forward a few steps. "Enough, Hack. Keep your hands off the gal.

Stealin's one thing. Harming a lady is something the boss won't abide."

"Honor amongst thieves?" Mr. Devers flashed a scornful glance.

The leader leveled his pistol at Mr. Devers again. "Don't press your luck, mister. I'm getting tired of you." He turned to his men. "Unhitch the team and let's ride."

They took off up the road leading the team, harness traces and reins flapping. Dust swirled and plumed behind them. Soon they were out of sight over the hill.

Clara released a long breath. Her hands found the solid lump in the bottom of her small handbag, and she tried to reassure herself that she would've been able to pull out the knife to protect herself if that outlaw had succeeded in getting her into the bushes. Perhaps she should carry it in her pocket from now on. "Thank you for defending me, Mr. Devers."

Sparks spit again and kicked at the dirt.

The messenger climbed up to check the box, as if hoping some of the money remained.

Mr. Devers dabbed his lip with a white handkerchief. "Are you all right, Miss Bainbridge?"

Clara nodded. "We should check on the driver." She started down the hill the way they'd come. "And one of you should go get the horses."

"The horses? They're long gone." Mr. Devers frowned, staring up the road where they had disappeared.

"I doubt it. They're still harnessed together, and they had a long run during the chase. Those outlaws won't want to be slowed down taking them along. You'll probably find the team over the next rise waiting for you." She kept walking.

The driver lay in the middle of the road a hundred yards away, unmoving. Mr. Devers and Sparks came with her, leaving the messenger to search for the team.

❧

Clara was coming home.

Alec McConnell tugged at his gloves. Sweat trickled down his back. Dust and grass clung to his skin. He gripped the weathered handle of the pitchfork and tossed another bundle of hay up the slippery pile in the loft. He buried the tines in the tumbled fodder again, leaning away from the weight to throw the next forkful high. Of all the pressing things on his list to do today, pitching up loose hay and tidying the haymow didn't even make the top dozen. So why was he up here sweltering under the eaves?

Twenty-four years old and hiding in the loft like a scared six-year-old. Certainly not acting like a grown man, a ranch foreman. Not that he'd been foreman for long.

A whole year. A year of being a foreman. A year since Mrs. Bainbridge died. A year since Clara left. Though he'd known the day of her return was fast approaching, he hadn't dealt with any of the feelings her homecoming caused to lope around inside him.

He'd missed her, missed the way she tried to boss them all around, missed her happy laughter, her baby blue eyes pleading with him not to tell her father of some misdeed. He missed her freckles and the smile that seemed too wide for her heart-shaped face. His lips twisted up at the corner. He must be out of his head, but he even missed her occasional bouts of temper, storming through the ranch house bent on righting some wrong.

Alec lifted another forkful, using his shoulders and arms to heave. His aim was a bit off, and hay slid back down the pile to his feet. The air pressed in, stifling hot, unusual for this early in the spring. He wiped his face with his shirttail and sat on a crate, breathing in dried-grass and old-wood smells.

Had that fancy ladies' school changed her much? Her

letters to her father—tomes the size of a family Bible— sounded like the same old Clara. How Alec had looked forward to the arrival of one of those monthly missives and the way the Colonel carried them around, reading bits aloud.

Mule-stubborn, steel-true, blade-straight. All the things that were Clara Bainbridge. Generous, impulsive, loving. And off limits. At least to the likes of him.

His youngest brother, Cal, stuck his head through the floor opening in the corner. "Hey, you done yet? It's almost time to go."

Alec waved his hand. "Almost, though why we're all going is beyond me." He adopted a stance of indifference, as he always did when the subject of Clara came up. Somehow, if he distanced himself, pretended he didn't care, talking about her didn't hurt as much. "I don't like town."

"Well, I'd have to say the feeling's pretty mutual, and you haven't done anything in recent memory to change those feelings. When are you going to let all that go?" Cal clambered the rest of the way up the ladder and swung into the loft. "But not go meet her stage? What kind of talk is that? She'll be mighty hurt if we aren't all there to greet her. The Colonel's pacing the porch now waiting for the wagon. I know you'd rather be skinned than show up in Money Creek these days, but this is a special occasion."

Clara had always treated Alec's siblings, Cal and Trace, like the brothers she never had. At one time, she'd treated Alec like a brother, too. When had her feelings changed? Or was it only Alec's feelings that had changed?

Cal tipped his battered Stetson back on his head, revealing short sandy hair. His blue eyes raked over Alec. "I don't understand you. You and Clara were the best of friends. But ever since she's been gone, you never want to talk about her. You go silent as a cigar-store Indian, or you growl at people like a bear with a chapped behind."

Alec kicked at the loose hay littering the floor. "I do not. Anyway, somebody has to stay here and get some work done. This ranch doesn't run itself. I don't have time for trips into town every day." Had Cal never guessed Alec's feelings for Clara?

"That's bunkum, and you know it. You sweat your guts out on this ranch from dawn till dark six days a week. You work harder than if it was your own spread." Cal grabbed another pitchfork leaning against the wall and thrust it into the pile. "Why do you drive yourself so hard? It's more than the Colonel expects."

Alec peeled off his gloves and stuck them in his back pocket. "You know why—because I owe him. You, me, and Trace would all be dead or in jail if it wasn't for him. I'm just trying to pay him back."

And maybe prove to myself and to him that I'm good enough to court his daughter? Naw, that will never happen, and it's plumb foolish to even think it. Clara Bainbridge deserved much better than anything Alec could offer her.

"The Colonel doesn't expect us to pay him back. And you couldn't, even if you spent every last day of your life on the Cross B and worked yourself to powder." Cal swept off his hat and whacked it on his thigh, releasing a cloud of dust. "Anyway, let's stop palavering and get into town. You know you wouldn't miss her homecoming, no matter how much work piled up around here."

Alec grimaced. His brother was right. He'd never miss Clara's homecoming. Painful as it might be.

two

"They're late." Alec paced the boardwalk in front of the freight office.

"Quit stewing. It's only an hour overdue." Cal lounged in the doorway. "And we made the most of the extra time by loading all that stuff she shipped ahead. This way we can take right off when she gets here." The laden wagon waited in the street, the patient team swishing flies and dozing in the spring sun.

"Where'd the Colonel go? And Trace?" He looked over his shoulder for his employer and the tall, silent, middle McConnell brother.

"Trace went to the gunsmith's, and the Colonel went to Purdy's to get some cinnamon candy for Clara. You know how much she likes that stuff."

Alec leaned against the hitching post. He rubbed the muzzles of the team, all the while looking down the south road for a telltale plume of dust. How many times had he bought cinnamon stick candy for Clara? A smile tugged at his lips. Every time he went to town. And every time he got home it was the same—his pretending he'd forgotten and her pestering the life out of him until he handed it over. Those had been the best times, when she'd still been a kid. Before the Colonel sent her to Boston. Before Alec had ruined everything by noticing Clara had grown up. Before he had fallen in love with her.

Alec had never told Clara of his feelings. What was the use? He couldn't and wouldn't act on them, so why let anyone know what was in his heart? A man had his pride, after all, though a McConnell had precious little to boast about and plenty to be ashamed of.

Alec hadn't bought cinnamon candy since Clara left.

"Quit frowning. It isn't Clara's fault the stage is late, and you glaring at the horizon isn't going to make it come any faster." Cal sauntered over to squint up the road. "You're jumpy as a june bug in a skillet. Let's go get a cup of coffee."

The Rusty Bucket Café, as dumpy as the name sounded, boasted the best meals in Money Creek, or in all of southern Idaho Territory. Cheap and filling, with a bottomless cup of coffee strong enough to dissolve a horseshoe and lately serving the best pie he'd ever tasted—though he didn't think he could face a piece right now—it was one of the few places in town Alec felt comfortable. He pushed through the front door, setting the bell to jangling.

They were halfway across the dining room when a hand reached out and grabbed his arm.

"Sit here, boys. I been meaning to head over to your place. Wanted to talk to you."

Seb Lewis cradled a mug of coffee. His clothes hung on his gaunt frame. He looked like a stiff breeze would knock him over. Alec had never seen him so used up.

"Howdy, Seb." Cal pulled out a chair and straddled it backward, crossing his arms on the back and resting his chin on his stacked wrists. "How're things over at the Double Box? You're looking a bit worn down at the heel." Seb barely scratched a living on the Double Box, doing the work of three cowboys himself with only one hired man to help him.

The proprietress, a woman who rivaled a buffalo for size, plunked down two enamel cups and a spatterware coffeepot. "What'll it be?" A pencil jutted from the back of her wild, orange hair, and a couple yards of calico apron stretched across her front.

"Just coffee, Georgia." Cal smiled, his eyes twinkling. "And maybe a slice of pie?"

As always, Cal's grin melted her caustic manners. "Sugar, when I heard Clara was comin' home today, I figured you'd be in town, so I saved the last slice of sour cream and raisin pie just for you. I had to hide it. Ever since Lily took over the baking, her sour cream and raisin pie just about flies off the pantry shelf."

Alec shook his head, a frown tugging at his mouth. Any woman from eight to eighty fell all over herself when Cal showed up. "I'll just have coffee, Georgia."

Seb perked up. "Why didn't you say you had sour cream pie left? I'll take a slice, too."

"You'll get dried apple, or you'll get none at all. I told you I saved the last piece for Cal." She bustled toward the kitchen, nose high.

Cal winked at Alec and poured the coffee. Alec braced himself before he took a sip. He was pretty sure Georgia threw a handful of roofing nails into every pot to settle the grounds.

She returned, crisscrossing the dining room, a tray held high. She set a plate before Cal like she was serving Governor Irwin himself. Dark raisins dotted the pale cream slice.

"Ah, Georgia"—Cal tucked his napkin into his shirt—"you know the way to my heart."

She giggled, her hair bristling aggressively. "Anything else you need, Sugar, you just holler." She plopped Seb's apple pie down without looking at him.

When she'd headed toward the kitchen, Alec put his elbows on the table. "What'd you want to talk about, Seb?"

"Cattle. You missing any?" He turned his pie plate around with a gnarled hand until the point of syrupy apples and flaky crust faced him.

Cal started, as always, on the crust end of his piece of pie, piercing a forkful and raising it to his mouth. He quirked an eyebrow at Alec.

Alec shrugged. "We always lose a few to winterkill, but we won't know how many until we start the roundup."

"We started roundup this week. I'm finding pockets of cattle here and there, but nowhere near as many as I'd hoped. I can't afford to lose any head." Seb stared at Alec, his eyebrows tenting in concern.

"It was a pretty mild winter. Maybe they just ranged up farther into the breaks than they have in previous years." Alec tucked his thumbs into his belt loops and tipped his chair back. He hooked a boot heel over the chair rung. They'd lost a cow or two to some hungry saddle tramp passing through, but in his three years at the Cross B, they hadn't suffered from any serious rustling. The Cross B and Double Box, lying deep in Money Creek Canyon with the only access right past the Colonel's front door, made rustling impossible.

Seb shrugged. "Maybe. But I've got a bad feeling."

Alec frowned. He couldn't afford to be missing any cows. Bainbridge had a contract with the army to supply beef to Fort Boise. And anything they had left over went to feed the miners over at Silver City. "You thinking predators got at 'em? We had some trouble with mountain lions last fall."

"Maybe," he said again. "Wolves might have scattered the herd, too. But this feels like more than predators."

Alec swirled the black sludge in the bottom of his cup. "We'll keep an eye out for Double Box cows. Maybe they mixed in with ours. They might have wandered up our way. If they're in with the Cross B herd, we'll cut 'em out and drive 'em back when we're done rounding up our stock."

Seb poked around his teeth with a toothpick. He nodded, ruminating. "You're probably right. Mild winter and a hot, dry spring. They're drifting toward the creek." He pushed back his empty plate. "Best pie in town, even if it wasn't sour cream raisin. And how do you like yours, Sugar?" He batted his eyes at Cal, imitating Georgia.

Cal licked his fork and laid it on the table. He leaned back and patted his stomach. "You're just jealous. You know she won't give you the time of day, no matter how hard you try." He grinned.

Seb shook his head, chuckling. "You all set for Clara's party?"

Alec reached for a toothpick from the little pot on the table and rolled it between his fingers. "The Colonel had us build a dance floor outside. And he's been grain-feeding a steer since the first of the year. He's invited the whole town. Should be some shindig. You're coming, aren't you?"

"Wouldn't miss it. You boys will have to kill more than one grain-fed steer to feed the crowd," Seb said.

Alec checked his watch. Where was that stage? The coffee gurgled in his tense stomach. Unease tickled the back of his neck. "We'd best get over to the station. They might've had word about the stage by now. And the Colonel will be waiting for us." He dug in his vest pocket and pulled out a few coins. "I'll get yours, Seb."

"You leaving already, Sugar?" Georgia stopped at their table, a large tray of meals balanced on her shoulder. She ignored Alec, focusing on Cal.

He sent her his best you're-the-only-woman-in-the-world smile. " 'Fraid so, Georgia. But that was some mighty fine pie."

"Tomorrow Lily's making pecan. I'll save you a piece."

"I'll think up some reason why I need to come to town." He winked at her.

She blushed and pushed past to serve her customers.

Alec rolled his eyes and headed for the door. "Why do you do that?"

Cal followed on his heels. "Do what?"

"Flirt and make a fuss over someone you're not interested in and wouldn't court in a month of Sundays?" He tossed a look over his shoulder.

Cal shrugged and settled his hat before edging past Alec out the door. "It makes her feel good. She knows it isn't serious. It's just a game."

"Hmph. It won't be much of a game if some girl gets her heart broken. It's making promises you don't intend to keep. Just like Pa."

The wide grin on Cal's face disappeared. "I'm nothing like him, and you know it." His hands fisted, a dull flush climbing his cheeks. "You take that back."

Alec backed up a step on the boardwalk, assessing his younger brother. "All right, I take it back, but you know it yourself that we all have to guard against acting like him. It's in the blood."

"Maybe it's in your blood, but I won't let it be in mine."

Alec looked down at his stocky, powerful younger brother, more like their fair mother—God rest her soul—in looks than the darker Trace or himself. The anger and resentment each man felt for their failure of a father came out in different ways. But it came out in all of them.

"Stage is coming!"

Relief and anxiety wrestled their way up Alec's spine. He pulled his hat low and stalked across the street to the freight office steps, glad to be free of thinking and talking about their father.

"She's coming mighty slow." Cal squinted up the Elko road.

The horses plodded, heads down. As one, Alec and Cal headed up the street.

Cal whistled. "That isn't Charlie at the reins."

The knot in Alec's stomach tightened. *Please, Lord, let*

Clara be all right.

The driver pulled the team to a stop in the middle of the road. The horses' heads hung low, sides heaving.

Alec could make out bright, splintered holes in the red paint of the coach. He broke into a run. His boots skidded in the dirt as he grabbed for the door handle. He wrenched it open, heart in his throat.

Clara's blue eyes, wide with surprise, stared into his. Breath rushed back into his lungs. Then he saw the blood. A man lay slumped beside her on the bench, and she held a cloth to his cheek. Bloodstained bandages wrapped his left arm. Red droplets scattered across her skirt. Two other men sat on the opposite seat, one sporting a darkening bruise on his jaw.

"What happened?"

"Alec." She smiled her sweet, gentle, shoot-him-through-the-heart smile.

The sound of his name on her lips after such a long time hit him like the kick of a mule. Everything he felt for her and all the reasons why he couldn't have her slammed together in his chest. He swallowed hard.

Nothing had changed. Had he really thought it would?

three

The sight of Alec's face was at once painful and joyous. He looked the same, and yet, different—older, certainly, but sadder, too, more careworn. His tanned skin bore white wrinkles beside his brown eyes. Chocolate brown hair curled at his nape under his sweat-stained hat. Clara's lips trembled. All her time away hadn't changed her feelings for him one bit.

Cal poked his head through the other door. "Hey, Clara, you all right?"

She pulled her gaze away from Alec to smile at Cal. "I'm fine, but we ran into a bit of trouble. The driver needs a doctor."

Clara waited until helpful hands lifted the injured man, and then she moved toward the door. Her legs and back protested being cramped into one position so long.

Mr. Devers stepped in front of Alec and Cal and offered his hand to assist her.

Trace arrived as her feet touched the road. He halted, looking at the bullet holes in the stage and the blood on her skirt.

She smiled to reassure him.

Cal shouldered Mr. Devers and Trace aside and swept her up into a mighty hug, lifting her from the ground and squeezing the air out of her. "I'm sure glad you're home. The place hasn't been the same since you left." He set her down and gave her another hug.

Trace pushed Cal away and took both of Clara's hands in his.

She blinked hard, gazing up into his familiar and beloved face. "Look at you. That moustache makes you look so distinguished."

Dark-haired, with smoke gray eyes, Trace was a man of few words. He squeezed her fingers, his eyes narrowing as he appraised her. "Welcome home, Clara." His voice·rolled over her, rusty and deep.

She withdrew her hands and reached up to embrace him, placing a peck on his cheek.

A ghost of a smile lifted one corner of his mouth. He nodded and stepped back.

"Clara."

She turned to greet her father. The Colonel hurried out of the stage office, walking stick tucked under his arm. He opened his arms, and she went into them, tears stinging her eyes. Stern, intimidating to most men, the Colonel enveloped her in his embrace. The familiar scents of hair oil and peppermint welcomed her home.

When he released her, he dug in his coat pocket. "Got you something, girl." He smiled and handed over the brown-wrapped bundle. She took one look at the cinnamon stick candy inside and hugged him again. Her homecoming was everything she'd imagined it would be. With one notable exception.

Alec leaned one shoulder against the side of the stage, arms crossed. His shirt stretched across his broad chest, and the brim of his hat shaded his face. Her heart bumped against her ribs at his intense appraisal. He could still take her breath away just by looking at her.

"Miss Bainbridge, I believe this is yours." The cultured voice of Mr. Devers yanked her attention away from Alec.

She turned to him.

He held out her valise.

"Oh, thank you. Where are my manners? Father, this is Mr. Devers. I owe him a debt of gratitude. He put himself into harm's way for me during the robbery."

The Colonel put out his hand. "Sir, I'm much obliged."

"Please, call me Steadman. I couldn't bear to see those ruffians mistreat a lady, especially one as charming as your daughter." His eyes slid sideways to look at her, his white teeth gleaming.

Warmth tinged Clara's cheeks, and she looked down at her hands.

The Colonel, though long retired, still carried himself with a military bearing. "I'm very grateful. Are you staying in the area long? We'd be delighted if you could come to supper some night soon."

"Actually, I've finally come to claim my ranch property. I purchased the Lazy P Ranch some time ago, but business prevented me from seeing my acquisition until now. Perhaps you've met my foreman, Mr. Sparks? He's been managing the property this past eighteen months."

The Colonel shook hands with Sparks. "Mr. Sparks, we don't run into you often. You must keep busy over that way."

Clara flicked a glance at Sparks. So that's why he'd seemed vaguely familiar this morning when they boarded the stage in Elko. She must've seen him around Money Creek before being sent to Boston. She lifted her gaze to Steadman's. "The Lazy P adjoins our property. Well, sort of. If it wasn't for the Stovepipe Hills between our ranch and yours, you could just about see my house from your front porch."

Steadman smiled. "The Stovepipe Hills? How quaint. And is there a quick way to cross those hills, so I might see you again soon, Miss Bainbridge?"

She flushed at his bold manner, knowing her father and the McConnell men—Alec—heard every word. "You may call me Clara. I'm afraid there is no easy way to cross the Stovepipes. That's rather rough territory. You have to travel around them, almost into town. Your ranch lies in the valley to the east of the ridge, while we're on the west side." Clara had an idea. "We're having a party at our place on Saturday, sort of a welcome home affair. It would be a nice way for you to meet folks, and a way for us to say thank you for what you did for me on the stage. Do say you'll come."

"I'd be delighted." He lifted her hand and kissed the air over her knuckles. How Continental, quite out of place in Money Creek. She wondered if he would last in rough-and-tumble Idaho Territory.

Cal shuffled close. "We'd best get over to the sheriff's office so you can report the robbery. He might want to gather a posse to go after them."

Trace took her valise for her, his steel-hard eyes measuring Steadman Devers. She suppressed a laugh. Not much had changed in a year. The boys still assumed the role of guardians, suspicious of any man who paid her the least attention.

"Good-bye, Steadman. I look forward to seeing you again." She slipped her arm through her father's, ignoring the scowl settled on Alec's features.

❧

Alec trailed behind them, trying not to watch the gentle sway of Clara's skirts and the way the sun glinted off her brown hair. The thought of Clara in danger scared him so bad his knees felt like biscuit dough.

Why had she let that Devers fellow fawn all over her? Kissing her hand? Just what had happened out there on the stage road? An emotion he refused to name rose up and colored the world green.

Alec strode fast and passed Clara, leaping up to the boardwalk in front of the jail to hold the door for her.

The sheriff's boots dropped off the desktop and his chair righted. "McConnell"—Sheriff Powers didn't quite spit the name, but he looked as if it tasted bad on his tongue—"if you're here about your pa, you can forget it. He's staying in jail until he's sobered up." He looked beyond Alec. "Why, Miss Clara, you've come back." He held out his hand to her, smiling. Sheriff Powers had been the law in this part of Idaho Territory for almost a decade, since just before Alec's mother and sister had died of cholera. Alec had never truly forgiven the man for burning the McConnell cabin to the ground that cold, October day. The sheriff's face hardened when he turned back to Alec. "The old man stays where he is."

Alec held his temper. "Clara is here to report a robbery." He positioned himself where he could watch her without being in her direct line of sight. Light from the front window played on her face. The vise that had clenched his heart since he first saw her tightened another notch.

"Powers!" The slurred shout came from the cells in the back of the jail. Alec stifled a groan. *Please, Lord, let him pass out and be quiet.*

"Powers, you sorry excuse for a lawman, let me outta here!" A skinny, filthy arm poked through the bars, a grasping, emaciated claw. "I'll rip out your liver!"

"Shut up, Gus!" Powers rose and stalked to the dividing door to the cells and slammed it shut, then hitched up his gun belt under his protruding middle. "Sorry about that, Miss Clara." He turned to Alec. "And don't you give me any trouble either. It wasn't so awful long ago I had you in that same cell for stealing. Your pa's a menace. I found him sneaking into the back of the Golden Slipper, drunk as a pie-eyed polecat and trying to steal a bottle of rye."

Muffled shouts leaked around the solid door's edge. Alec stared at the floor, taking deep breaths to calm his rising anger. Powers took great joy in reminding Alec and anyone else who would listen that Alec had a past as a petty thief and firebrand. Shame shot through Alec and settled in his gut. He'd never live down his past in this town. One of those thieving McConnells. Did it matter that his indiscretions had been more than three years ago? Did it matter that he'd changed? That he'd repented of his sins? That he'd asked for and received forgiveness from God and made restitution for the things he'd stolen? "No trouble, Sheriff. Leave him in there till he rots. Go ahead, Clara, so we can get out of here." He refused to look at Trace or Cal, who had also spent time in Powers's jail in the past— before the Colonel and Mrs. Bainbridge had rescued them all and showed them a better way.

Clara answered the sheriff's questions without hesitation, and halfway through her recounting, the stage messenger came in from delivering the driver to the doctor's and corroborated her story. Clara kept her answers clear and concise. "There were six of them. About ten miles down the Elko road. They all wore bandanas, and I didn't recognize any of them. One of the men is named Hack. At least that's what the leader called him. He rode a shaggy pinto, black and white. They took the payroll, Mr. Devers's wallet, and Mr. Sparks's moneybag as well. They started to take me, too, but Mr. Devers stepped in."

Alec closed his eyes, his fists clenching until his fingers ached. Six outlaws? All pointing guns at her, and there she sat, chattering like she was at Sunday supper, not a care in the world. Didn't have the sense God gave a prairie chicken. A year back East had stolen her ability to see danger when it was screaming in her face.

"Who was driving?" The sheriff wrote down her statement in a cramped hand, laboring over the page like a schoolboy.

"Charlie Francis." The messenger gave the information. "Gunshot to the arm and a crease on the face. He's a good driver. Drinks now and again, but not on the job."

Powers nodded and rubbed his fingertips against his thumb and stuck his lips out as if considering this news. "Well, Miss

Clara, thank you for reporting this. You've given us plenty to go on, but if I think of anything else to ask, I'll ride out to the ranch. And if you think of anything, send for me. I guess I'd better get word to Silver City and let them know the money's been stolen." He shook his head. "I'll take my deputies out and have a look around, see if I can pick up a trail." He didn't sound as if he had much hope. "This is the third stage robbery since the roads opened this spring. McConnell, can you ride with us?" He looked at Trace.

Alec pressed his tongue hard against his front teeth. They were all "McConnell" to Powers, as they were to most of the town. Not individual men, just "McConnell."

Trace nodded. He took out his pistol and checked the load. "Got my horse out front. And my rifle's on my saddle."

Alec glared at the sheriff, biting back all he wanted to say. Powers didn't like the McConnells, but he wasn't above using them if he thought it necessary. He'd risk Trace's neck in a manhunt, but he wouldn't greet him in church on Sunday.

"Trace, you will be careful?" Clara looked up at him with pleading eyes.

He winked at her. "I'm always careful."

Alec led the way from the sheriff's office, eager to get out of there. The short walk to where the horses were tied did nothing to soothe him. He yanked the reins from the hitching post, making his horse, Smoke, snort and dance back.

"Alec insisted we bring Hawkwing." Her father directed Clara toward the wagon with his hand on the small of her back. "He thought you'd want to ride the rest of the way after being cooped up in the stage. I told him you'd be different now that you'd had proper schooling, and you'd want to ride in the wagon."

Clara stopped, her brows coming together. "Father, that's

very kind of you, but I really would prefer to ride. It's been such a long time."

"But, Clara—" The Colonel broke off when Clara rushed away from him toward the horses.

Alec took a step back as she threw her arms around the bay's neck, burying her face in his mane. Hawkwing nuzzled her and whinnied. "I've missed you so much." She gave the horse a once-over. Her hand trailed over her saddle, shiny in the sunlight, and the satiny burnish of Hawkwing's hindquarters. He swished his glossy, black tail. "He looks fine, Father." She smiled at the Colonel. "You took good care of him, just like I asked in my letters."

The Colonel dug in his vest pocket, withdrawing his watch for a quick glance. "It wasn't me. Alec saw to him. Are you sure you wouldn't rather go with Cal and me?"

"Oh no, Father. I want to ride. It's been such a long time. I'll be careful."

Cal climbed aboard the wagon and picked up the reins. "I thought Alec was going to rub the hair right off old Hawkwing, he brushed him so often. Rode him every now and again, too, so he wouldn't get too fresh."

Alec held Hawkwing's reins and helped Clara mount, wishing Cal would shut up. Touching her felt like grabbing a lightning bolt. He avoided her look, afraid she would see right into his heart. He didn't want her to guess he'd lavished attention on her horse in an effort to be less lonely for her while she was away. "Let's ride. Chores are waiting." He swung aboard Smoke and pointed the gray gelding toward the Cross B Ranch.

Clara's pink skirts spread over her mount's flanks. She was too pretty for her own good.

Six outlaws. He clamped his jaw tight.

"Alec?"

He glanced at her then looked ahead.

"Thank you for taking such good care of my horse."

He nodded and put the lid on the pot of might-have-been feelings bubbling in his chest and pointed his horse south for the hour-long ride home.

Clara stayed close to the wagon and kept up a string of chatter with Cal and the Colonel. Alec listened more to the sound than to the words, a smile tugging at his lips. The ranch had been a mighty quiet place with her gone.

They followed Money Creek along the valley floor for miles until the ranch buildings finally came into view.

Clara pulled Hawkwing up beside the wagon and sat still, soaking in the view. "I can't tell you how good it is to be home. I've missed all of this and all of you so much." She held her hand out to her father and swallowed hard. "I know you and Mama always planned for me to go to school back East. I just wish it hadn't come right on the heels of—" Her lips trembled. "Anyway, I'm home to stay now."

She rode sedately beside the wagon all the way down the slope. Alec missed the little hoyden she had been, always racing around on horseback, following in her mother's tracks. After Mrs. Bainbridge's death in a riding accident and a year in a finishing school in Boston, she'd grown up a lot it seemed.

They pulled up in front of the ranch house, which sported a new coat of paint in honor of her return. Alec watched her step onto the porch then turned toward the barn. Like always, he had a lot to do before dark. At least work kept a man from thinking too much.

Halfway to the corral, one of the hands met him. "Boss, someone left the gate open. Champ got into the grain. I think he's foundered." Alec sprinted for the barn, shouting for Cal and the Colonel as he ran.

four

Clara stood still for a moment, watching the retreating backs. Home for exactly three minutes and already abandoned. She smiled. The ranch—first, last, and always.

She walked back down the steps to the wagon. Standing on tiptoe, she peered over the side. There, the valise she sought huddled between a bag of feed and a crate of what appeared to be windmill parts. She wrenched the bag out and turned to hurry inside.

Clara went to her room at the head of the stairs and quickly removed her traveling costume. She opened the wardrobe, running her fingers over the sturdy ranch clothes she had worn before her exile to Boston. A serviceable ivory blouse and faded blue riding skirt would do.

She brushed the snarls from her hair and parted the thick tresses into three hanks, braiding them quickly. Rather than waste time pinning it up, she let the braid swing down her back. Sliding into her boots, she couldn't help a smile. Such footgear was a necessity here, but oh, the scandalous looks they would garner back East. Her heels clomped on the stairs in a satisfying reminder that she was finally home.

She paused at the head of the stairs, steeling herself for a look into the master bedroom. A hard lump formed in her throat and longing swept over her. Being sent away from home only two weeks after losing her mama meant Clara hadn't worked through a lot of the emotions and "firsts" she would've if she'd stayed home. Now, a year removed from the tragedy, it felt as fresh and new as if it were just the day before.

The changes to the room were subtle but sharp all the same. Her mother's dressing table was bare, as was the top of the wardrobe where she'd always kept her hatboxes. Father had written to say he was putting all of Mama's things into the spare room for Clara to sort through when she got home. Clara didn't know if she'd be able to anytime soon.

Once inside the cavernous barn, she let her eyes adjust to the gloom. A knot of men stood in the open back door around an iron gray stallion. The horse stood awkwardly, his hind legs bunched under his body, his forelegs poking out, as if he wanted to bear all his weight on his heels. His coat dripped with sweat, his ears lay pinned back against his head, and saliva hung in a rope from his open jaws. As she neared, she could hear his grunting breath and the occasional groan as he shifted his weight.

"Clara, what are you doing out here? A barn is no place for a lady." Her father's brows came down. He moved to stand between her and Champion.

"What's come over you, Father? I used to spend more time in the barns than in the house." She stepped to his side and threaded her arm through his.

"That was a long time ago. You're a grown woman, and I'm sure you didn't hang out in the stables at the school in Boston. You should be resting after your long trip."

Clara laughed and squeezed his arm. "Really, you don't have to coddle me." She turned to focus on the horse.

Alec ran his hand along the crest of the horse's mane, trying to soothe the animal's distress. "How much of the mineral spirits did you get into him?"

The Colonel studied the bottle. "There's about half left."

"Worst case of founder I've ever seen." Cal squatted by Champ's front feet and placed his palm against one black hoof. The horse jerked away. "Hotter'n a stove lid."

The horse groaned again. The Colonel blew out a breath. "We best get him to the creek. It's the only hope for him."

The Colonel took the lead rope while Alec and Cal locked their arms behind the horse's back legs. Pulling and pushing, they forced the agonized stallion through the barn and down the slope toward Money Creek.

Clara bit her lip, gripping her hands tight at her waist. The poor animal wheezed, his flanks coated with sweat.

Halfway down the slope, they stopped to let Champion catch his breath. Alec rubbed the edge of his fist against the pale star between the stallion's eyes and fiddled with the sweat-soaked forelock. All the while he murmured reassurances.

Clara's heart swelled. She envied the special bond Alec had with horses. She loved Hawkwing but couldn't communicate with him the way Alec seemed to with any horse he met.

Alec stepped back. "Let's go." This time it was harder to get Champion moving. He fought the rope, legs spraddled, white ringing his eyes. His sides bellowed with his harsh breathing.

"Can't we let him rest a bit longer?" Clara directed her question to Alec. "He's in so much pain."

"If we don't get those hooves cooled off, he'll have to be put down. His hooves will slough off, and his legs will become deformed." The muscles worked in his jaw as he battled the horse. "There's not a lot we can do, but the cold water might help."

Cal finally had to smack the horse on the rump with the flat of his hand and let out a piercing whistle. Champion bolted. Twice, Clara thought he might go down, but he rallied and kept his feet. He hovered on the creek bank. Alec took the lead rope and plowed into the water. With Cal and the Colonel pushing, they forced Champ into the stream.

Men and beast puffed, catching their breaths. Champion trembled from head to foot, head hanging, his muzzle almost in the knee-high water. He ignored the men, focused only on his misery.

Alec and Cal leapt out of the water. Cal laughingly swiped water from his cheeks and chin. "I took a tumble there at the end. Think I soaked up half of Money Creek." He squeezed the hem of his shirt and shook his head, sending droplets flying.

Alec flopped down and tugged at his boot.

When the wet leather wouldn't budge, Clara hurried forward. "Let me."

❧

The last thing Alec wanted was for Clara to get closer. He barely kept himself from scooting backward on the ground and tried to appear casual. "I'm fine." He could just about maintain his indifference if she kept her distance. Seeing her in familiar garb, her hair hanging like a rope down her back, caused his heart to knock around like a pebble in a canning jar.

"Don't be silly. Your boots have to be full of icy water." She seemed not to notice his skittishness, for she advanced, grabbed his foot, and yanked.

The boot slid off and landed on the ground with a thump. In spite of the chilly dousing, heat bloomed through him when he caught sight of his big toe poking out of a hole in his sodden sock. He snatched his foot back and grabbed for his boot. Pouring out a stream of water, he kept his eyes on the ground. Before he could protest further, she had his other boot off.

"You really should change. You'll catch cold walking about with wet feet." Her brows bent down with concern.

"Hey, what about me?" Cal indicated his own sopping person. "Old Alec only got his tootsies wet. I went in head-first. Don't I deserve a little fussing over?" He grinned at Clara, eyebrows high. Alec tugged on his boots to hide his bare toe—pulling hard when the wet leather stuck fast—and rose to stamp his feet all the way in.

The Colonel slid his watch out of his pocket. "Let him stand in the water for an hour then try to get him moving a little. From the looks of things, he ate nearly a bushel of corn out of the bin. More than enough to make him founder."

"Hello!" A shout sounded up the slope above them. Trace rode slowly toward them leading a horse and balancing a rider in the saddle.

Alec's innards turned as icy as his toes. What was Trace thinking bringing Pa out here? The horses neared. Alec shot a glare at Trace.

The Colonel tapped his chin, eyes sad, mouth twisted in a thoughtful quirk. "Trace, any sign of the stage robbers?"

Trace shook his head, keeping a strong grip on Pa's shoulder as he mumbled, head lolling. "Dunno. At the last minute, Powers told me he didn't need my help and told me to take charge of Pa. Said he and the posse would probably be out a couple of days, and he didn't have anyone to spare to keep an eye on the jail."

Alec glanced at Clara, who had her bottom lip tucked behind her top teeth and her arms crossed at the waist. She stared at Pa, eyebrows pinching together. A shaft of humiliation lanced Alec's chest. A giant weight pressed on his shoulders. The chasm between them widened another mile. How disgusted she must be.

Cal reached down and picked up a stone, firing it into the creek well away from Champion. His jaw muscle bulged, and the cords in his neck stood out. He never once looked at Pa swaying in the saddle. Anger flowed off him in waves.

Alec turned his back on his father and stared at the stallion. Champion had his head up a little more, and he no longer drooled, in too much distress to swallow. A tiny light had grown in his eye, as if things might be looking up for him after all.

Alec swept his hat from his head and crushed the brim. He had too many responsibilities here at the Cross B. He didn't need to be saddled with a drunken, belligerent father who'd never shown any true remorse for the life he'd led.

The Colonel put his hand on Clara's shoulder. "Let's go up to the house. Boys, you can bed your father down in the bunkhouse." He cast them a pitying glance that churned the acid in Alec's stomach.

Pity. The very thought of it made him want to punch something. He was grateful when the Colonel led Clara away toward the house. He glared at Trace.

Trace shrugged. "Couldn't just leave him there."

Cal wrinkled his nose. "He smells like a silage heap. We should dump him in the creek alongside the horse. That might sober him up."

Trace snorted. "Naw. Would probably kill the fish for ten miles down *and* upstream. But I couldn't leave him in the jail. He's a sick old man." Resignation hung from every word. "We'd best get him up to the bunkhouse."

"Not me." Cal rocketed another stone into the water. "I'm done with that old soak. I can't believe you brought him here, Trace. You should've just left him on the street. That's what he would've done if it was one of us."

Trace shook his head. "We aren't supposed to do to him like he did to us. We're supposed to do to him what we *wish* someone would do for us if we were in need. And anyway, it's what Ma would've wanted. It's what the Lord would want us to do, too."

Cal jerked his chin as if he'd been slapped. "Lot of good it did Ma to try to look after him. All it did was send her to an early grave, her and Priscilla, and leave us to fend for ourselves. Wish he'd have died instead of Ma."

Years of hurt, neglect, and abuse colored Cal's words. He was right. Angus McConnell had never had a thought for anyone but himself. But as much as Alec wanted to, he couldn't just dump his father on the ground and leave him.

Trace seemed to have infinite patience, the ability to go back over and over to help their father. Alec figured Cal had used up whatever patience he had long ago. And Alec struggled somewhere in the middle, hating all their father had done to them but sorry for him, too.

"Cal, you stay with the horse. I'll help Trace."

five

Clara crossed the broad porch and searched in vain for Alec in the crowd milling on the lawn. She wrapped her arm around a pillar and scanned the throngs gathered at the buffet tables. Wood smoke from the barbeque pit hung in the air. Music and conversation blended together. A very nice homecoming. Except that for the three days since her arrival, Alec had avoided her at every turn.

"Say, Miss Clara, this is some party. I think everybody in town showed up." A man she didn't know lifted his laden plate in a salute.

The Colonel edged around a group of laughing men. "Clara, more people are arriving. Come greet them with me on the steps." He took her arm and steered her through the guests to the porch stairs. "Are you enjoying yourself, my dear?"

"Yes, Father." Sort of. The party was very nice, but Alec's absence, at first a mild concern, now chafed. "Where are the boys?"

"Now, dear, don't worry about them. They had to go to the south pasture to fix the windmill. Something fouled the pump. They'll be back soon. I know they wouldn't miss your party. Ah, here's Mr. Devers." A smile sprang to her father's lips. "Steadman, so glad you could join us."

Clara stepped forward and offered her hand. "Steadman, welcome." He was as handsome as ever, hair and clothing immaculate. Behind him, Sparks hovered, rolling his hat brim in his hands. "And Mr. Sparks. How lovely."

"Miss, thanks for the invitation."

"Please, help yourselves to the refreshments." She indicated the laden tables. Seeing Steadman and Sparks brought back images of the stage robbery. Now that the sheriff and his posse had returned empty-handed, it irritated her that the robbers still enjoyed freedom.

The Colonel sidestepped a group of guests. "Steadman, how are you settling in over at the Lazy P?"

Steadman inclined his head. "I must confess, it's very different from anything I'm used to, but Sparks assures me he has everything under control. I'm quite enjoying my role as gentleman rancher. And the house is surprisingly comfortable. I hadn't anticipated anything so grand."

Clara followed the conversation on the surface, continually scanning the crowd for signs of the McConnell brothers.

The Colonel rubbed his moustache with his index finger. "The former owner sank a lot of his capital into the house. I hear it's beautiful, though not many have seen it. He mostly kept to himself."

"I hope to change the reputation of the Lazy P. And I'd like to return your hospitality, if I may. Please, come visit this week. I'd appreciate any advice you might have, though I have every confidence in Sparks as a foreman. But for now, I'm sure we must be boring Miss Bainbridge with our conversation." Steadman gave a broad smile. "No lady of such quality could possibly want to discuss ranching, especially not at her homecoming party."

The band, actually three Irishmen from the Silver Creek Mine, started another song. The violin and accordion nearly drowned out the guitar.

Steadman inclined his head. "With your permission, Colonel? Miss Bainbridge, would you do me the honor?"

Clara looked once more over the crowd, hoping to see Alec returning. How could he be out fixing a windmill during her homecoming party? Sometimes his dedication to the Cross B drove her mad.

Steadman showed her to the dance floor and helped her step up onto the boards. The fresh smell of pine resin rose up from beneath her feet. She allowed him to lead her in time to the music. He held her correctly, directing with confident pressure against her back. His strong fingers wrapped around hers, and he made no effort to draw her closer. Clara made a mental apology to her deportment instructor at the finishing school for all the trouble she'd given that fine lady. Matching Steadman's dancing ability more than made up for the hours of tedious practice.

She assessed Steadman's looks while trying not to stare. Hair neat, moustache trimmed, smelling of soap and starch. His suit—so unlike the homespun, buckskins, or denim of most of the men in this territory—fit him well, lying perfectly across his shoulders. Keenly aware of the curious glances coming their way, Clara was relieved Steadman held her at a proper distance. Such a gentleman. She put his age at somewhere between thirty and thirty-five. Urbane and confident and more like one of the Boston gentlemen of her recent acquaintance than a rancher.

The music ended, and his arms dropped away. They applauded lightly, but when the fiddle and squeezebox took up a toe-tapping melody, Steadman ushered her off the floor toward the punch bowl.

"I'm afraid my skills in the more rustic dance steps are not up to par."

The way he said "rustic dance steps" made Clara glance up at him. She could hardly blame him for not being overly impressed with a frontier gathering when he had probably been to much more elaborate parties back East.

Father appeared at her elbow with two glasses of punch,

which he offered to them. "Glad to see you having a good time, Clara. Steadman, I hope you're enjoying yourself."

"Indeed, sir. Your daughter's company is very enjoyable."

He stared at her so intently she grew uncomfortable. She dropped her gaze and turned to her father. "Have the boys returned?"

"They'll be back soon, I'm sure." He gave a dismissive wave. "I forgot to ask if you're keeping the ranch name."

"I just saw the sheriff today and informed him that I would be keeping the Lazy P brand. No sense duplicating work, I say. Sparks tells me it would take many man-hours to round up every cow just to change the brand." He shrugged. "Sparks is one of the hardest working men I've ever seen. He's in the saddle from dawn until dark, and sometimes later. I can't imagine him working any harder."

The Colonel pursed his lips, his toe tapping to the music, raising little puffs of dust. "A ranch takes a lot of work. I'm often away on business, so I leave a lot in the hands of my foreman." He nodded and waved when someone greeted him across the way. "I didn't know the previous owner had put the Lazy P on the market until the property was already sold. I'd have snapped it up myself. The only drawback to that is the Stovepipe Hills. Hill is a bit of a misnomer, isn't it? All canyons and ravines, too steep for grazing."

"The canyons do make quite a barrier between the two properties. It would be so much better if there was a way through between your ranch and mine." Devers inclined his head as the music rose to a crescendo.

Clara sipped her punch and watched for men on horseback coming in from the range. Still no sign of them.

Father shook his head. "It's foolishness to even try looking for a way through. That loose shale can be deadly."

Clara's heart constricted at his flat, emotionless tone. If

her mother hadn't been trying to find a way through the canyons, she never would've fallen to her death. Father had written her in Boston that he'd gone so far as to fence off the opening to Skull Canyon, the place where she died, to keep cattle and people out and hopefully prevent another death. Clara cast about for a change in topic. Before she could come up with anything, movement near the creek caught her eye. "It's them." Relief rushed through her. They hadn't missed the entire party.

Alec rode in the lead, his horse striding into the water, sending up silver sheets of spray. Cal and Trace followed behind, Trace leading a pack horse with tools strapped to the saddle.

When Clara would've gone to greet them, her father held her arm. "I'm sure they'd appreciate some time to clean up. Leave them be, and come with me. Steadman, I'd like you to meet someone."

An hour later, after several more dances and another glass of punch, Clara stood between Steadman and her father on the porch. If she had to listen to one more braggart blather on about his importance, she just might scream. She forced herself to concentrate on Mr. Tarrance's plans to expand his mining operation and tried to keep from looking past his shoulder toward the bunkhouse.

Trace and Cal had arrived, dressed in their best clean denims and buttoned shirts. Cal instantly had a bevy of girls, young and old, surrounding him. He smiled and laughed, his light tan cowboy hat easy to spot in the crowd. Trace stood off to the side, a cup of coffee in his hand, silent and watchful as always.

Finally, Alec stepped out of the bunkhouse. Clara's breath caught in her throat. He wore a white shirt that contrasted with his tanned skin and dark hair. When he walked into the late afternoon sunshine, he settled his hat on his head, the brim shading his expression. To her surprise, he headed straight for the barn.

Without even excusing herself, Clara lifted her hem and walked down the stairs. "Clara? Where are you going?" Her father's voice followed her. She didn't look back.

&

Alec leaned on Champion's stall door and watched the stallion. In the days since the animal had foundered, he'd made good progress. Still stiff-legged, but no longer in agonizing pain. Alec ducked his head to look at the horse's hooves. If they were lucky, they'd caught the laminitis in time, and Champion wouldn't have permanent hoof damage.

"So this is where you are."

He turned. Clara stood silhouetted in the barn doorway. Backlit like she was, he couldn't read her expression. His grip tightened on the stall door, his muscles going rigid.

She walked closer. He couldn't decide what color her dress was, some sort of peach or pink, with lots of lace trim and some ruffles. She had her hair all piled up in fancy swirls and ringlets. One shiny coil bounced against her cheek. She didn't stop walking until she was only a step away. "How is he doing?"

"Huh?"

She smiled and pointed. "How is Champion doing?" She smelled like flowers.

"Fine." Alec glanced over her shoulder through the doorway toward the house. "It looks like a nice party. You should be out there with your guests."

"So should you." She regarded him with those big, blue eyes.

His heart beat thick in his throat. Did she have any idea the effect she had on him? He shrugged. "It's pretty high-class. Lots of townsfolk."

She frowned. "Everyone was invited. There are cowboys,

miners, shopkeepers. . .why, Cal's dancing with Georgia from the café right this minute."

A chuckle forced its way out of his throat. "Cal better watch his step, or Georgia's going to drag him to the altar."

"He hasn't changed a bit, has he? Still carefree and un-attached." She tugged her bottom lip.

Alec watched, fascinated.

She stood on tiptoe to look into the stall. The rough wood of the partition contrasted with the smooth softness of her complexion. When she lifted her hands away from the stall door, one fingerless net glove snagged on a splinter. "Oh no." Her brows arrowed in displeasure.

"Here, let me." He stepped so close he could smell the sunshine in her hair. His fingers, though almost as rough as the wood, closed around her hand. He eased the lace off the sliver, freeing her.

She looked up at him, eyes wide. A fellow could drown in those eyes. His pulse jumped in his throat just under his jaw. He tried to swallow.

"Alec?" His name came out a whisper on her lips. She was like one of those Sirens of myth he'd read about once, calling to him, beckoning him to his destruction.

He couldn't bear it anymore. She was so dear, and so close. His hands stole upward to her shoulders, and his head inclined toward hers. Her lips were only a breath away. His eyes closed.

" 'Scuse me."

Alec jumped back, dropping his arms from about her. He whipped his head around, heart thundering.

Angus McConnell. Dear old dad.

Alec didn't know whether to punch him for barging in at such a moment or thank him for keeping Alec from making a complete fool of himself.

Pa twisted his hat in his hands. Hunch-shouldered, with

bloodshot eyes that glowed hot and empty in the falling dusk, he tottered in the open doorway. At least he wasn't drunk. He wore clean clothes, though they hung on his frame. Only forty-five, he looked twenty years older, skin wrinkled, blue eyes watery and pale.

He shuffled closer. Suffering from his overindulgence in drink, for the last three days he'd taken his vile temper out on anyone who ventured near. It had been a relief to ride out to work on the windmill and escape his tirade. But tonight, he was apologetic and sober. And a living, breathing reminder to Alec why he had to steer clear of Clara Bainbridge.

"Don't mean to interrupt." He bobbed his head at Clara. "But I'm wanting a few words with my son."

Alec swallowed and looked into Clara's confused eyes. A delicate flush climbed her cheeks. Of all the stupid things to do. What had he been thinking? A fine lady like Clara, being pawed by a McConnell, and in a barn of all places.

She looked from him to his father and back again. "Of course. And I should attend to my guests. Will I see you later, Alec?" He didn't blame her for wanting to flee.

He jerked his chin. She might see him later, but not alone, not if he could help it.

She lifted her hem and left, stopping at the door to cast a glance back over her shoulder.

Alec contemplated the rafters for a moment and then turned to his father. "What do you want?"

Pa grinned, his stained teeth showing. "Whooee, she's a looker. I had no idea you'd aimed so high. Colonel Bainbridge's daughter? Why, you'll be in clover if you hitch up with her."

"You're out of your mind. I'm not aiming anywhere."

"Not what it looked like to me." Another leer.

"Drop it. What did you want to talk to me about?"

"I want some money." Pa's back straightened an inch or two, and he glared, challenging Alec.

"No. You'll only spend it on whiskey." Alec shoved his hands into his pockets. "Go back to the bunkhouse."

"Don't you order me around, you pup. I'm a grown man, and I can take care of myself."

"If you're so good at taking care of yourself, why are you asking me for money?" Alec checked the latch on the stall door. "You taking care of yourself—that's a laugh. Like you were taking care of yourself when Trace got you out of jail and hauled you here? You didn't even know where you were, you were so pickled."

Pa sneered at Alec. "You shouldn't be so high and mighty. It isn't as if you haven't seen the inside of one of Powers's cells yourself. You always were an uppity youngster, thinking you were better than me. I should've cuffed you a few more times when you were younger. Might've made you respectful of your elders."

Alec's hands fisted, his body rigid. "You knocked all of us around more than enough."

"Quit sniveling. I want money."

"No. I don't have any money for liquor. And don't go asking Trace or Cal for any either. They know better."

Pa's eyes glittered with anger. He stood still for a moment, his narrow chest rising and falling. A fleck of saliva appeared at the corner of his mouth, and he swiped it away with the back of his hand. "I guess you'll have plenty of money if you catch that gal. Then maybe you'll spare your old pa a couple of dollars when he needs it."

A twinge of pity flicked Alec's conscience, and he softened his voice. "I'm not going to marry that gal, and I'm not going to give you any money. Why don't you let me fix you a plate of food from the party, and I'll bring it to you in the bunkhouse?"

"I don't want food. I want money. If you won't give it to me, I'll get it myself."

"The only way you could get money is to beg for it or steal it. The sheriff catches you doing either, you'll be right back in jail. And it won't be the Money Creek jail either. They'll send you to the territorial prison and put you on a work gang. How'd you like that, huh? Busting your back all day?" Alec's mouth went dry at the thought. A spell on a chain gang would probably kill Angus McConnell. And though Alec had little love for the man who had fathered him, he didn't want to see him dead. He felt himself weakening. Perhaps he should just give him some money. But he tightened his resolve. "Why don't you just dry out and quit giving in to the liquor? Don't you know what you're doing to yourself, and to us, every time you go on a bender? Folks already think McConnells are the lowest of the low, and you go around trying to prove them right."

Alec turned his back and stared out the way Clara had gone. What was she thinking right now? Was she embarrassed that he'd been so forward? Was she disgusted that a McConnell had dared even think about kissing her?

"Quit thinking about that Bainbridge gal. You've got time and aplenty to chase skirts later. Right now, I'm talking to you."

Always and only the conversation had to be about Angus and his needs. Alec spoke without turning around. "Get out. Go back to the bunkhouse. And don't you mention Clara's name again."

Angus shuffled away.

Alec leaned his forearms on the top of Champion's stall and dropped his head. Clara's face swam into his vision. So beautiful. Could she ever be his? But no. He wouldn't do that to her, ruin her reputation by associating her with the McConnell name. He had nothing to offer her, no property, no money, just a drunken father and a lousy reputation with the townsfolk. She deserved better than that, much better. And she didn't deserve to be trifled with and disappointed. He had to keep his distance.

Alec pounded his fists against the stall door. He had enough stupidity to fill two fools his size.

ᨠ

Clara returned to her guests, but her mind wasn't on being a good hostess. Instead, visions of Alec, a breath away from kissing her, filled her mind. Her heart soared. He did care for her. At last, he was on the verge of making his feelings known. If only his father hadn't interrupted. . .

She kept a watch on the barn door, waiting for him to reappear, to come to her, perhaps to ask her to dance. Wouldn't it be heavenly to be held in his arms?

Every nerve tingled, and she felt as though she could fly. Colors looked more vivid, sounds became sharper, the aroma of the roasting meat smelled better. The love she had for him, the love she'd held in check until he should declare himself, bloomed inside her until she was sure it must show on her face.

But he didn't come. She waited through dinner, speech-making, and singing by the campfire. She waited through saying good-bye to her guests and all through the clearing up. She waited so long, doubts eroded her certainty. Had she misunderstood? Had she somehow done something wrong that would make Alec stay away?

Clara lingered on the porch, watching the hands file into the bunkhouse.

Cal, at the tail end of the line, turned, lifted his lantern, and waved.

She wrapped her arms around herself to stave off a sudden chill that had nothing to do with the late evening breeze.

six

To his knowledge, no one had ever called Alec McConnell a coward, but he sure felt like one the morning after the party. Leading six Cross B cowboys—drooping in the saddle and yawning after their late night—he pointed his horse south, glad to have the excuse of the spring roundup to put the ranch house behind him.

Riley, Alec's big, shaggy cow dog, jogged along at Alec's stirrup, tongue lolling, tail wagging. His bright eyes took in everything. A cross between an Irish wolfhound and a mastiff, Riley was a powerful, formidable dog. His gnarled, gray fur resisted thorns and brambles, and his jaws, once they closed over the ear or nose of a cantankerous cow, locked like a bear trap. He roamed where he pleased, but with uncanny awareness, showed up whenever Alec needed him for work.

Cal rode beside his brother, emitting head-splitting yawns every few seconds. He rode relaxed, his wrists crossed on the saddle horn. "Why'd we have to leave so early?"

"This isn't early. We should've been underway an hour ago." Alec rolled his shoulders and neck and blinked his eyes against the rising sun. By the time he'd gotten back to the bunkhouse after a long walk beside the creek, Pa had been gone. No doubt he'd caught a ride with someone at the party back into town. Probably bummed some spare change off some tender soul, spent it all on a bottle of rotgut, and was now passed out or in the town jail again—or both. When the ranch hands finally returned to the bunkhouse just after midnight, joshing and laughing, Alec had rolled over in his bunk and pretended to be asleep.

He cast a glance back over his shoulder to the diminishing ranch house. Guilt sat like a sack of cannonballs in his stomach. He had a yellow streak a mile wide painted down his back, turning tail and running away last night, sneaking off this morning. Shrugging didn't alleviate the uneasiness. And he had no explanation to offer Clara for his absence. But it was better this way. He needed to stay away from her for her own good.

Off to Alec's right, the supply wagon rattled and rolled over the bumps. The cook leaned on his thighs, the lines loose between his fingers. Brilliant sunrays streamed over the jagged canyon tops on their left.

"Where do you plan to set up the first camp?" Cal blinked then rubbed his eye with the heel of his hand.

"That little oxbow near the mouth of Skull Canyon. Might as well start at the wildest part of the ranch and work toward the middle." Alec stared at the area between Smoke's swiveling ears. What was Clara doing at that moment? His heart hammered remembering the feel of her in his arms, the sweet headiness of her lips a hair's breadth from his. He shook his head, jarring the thought away.

Cal stood in his stirrups and looked across the valley floor to the east.

Sadness swept over Alec as he followed his brother's stare. An unmistakable rock formation jutted from the closest butte. Skull Canyon, fenced off since Mrs. Bainbridge had died there.

Cal shrugged and settled back into his saddle. "That was a bad day. I'll never forget the search."

Alec scowled, pushing down the memory of that terrible day. What good did it do to remember? She was dead. Thinking about it wouldn't bring her back. "Let's get a move on. Roundup isn't going to wait. You boys are all half asleep."

"You would be, too, if you'd had the decency to go to the party. Where were you anyway? You must've been the only cowboy in fifty miles who wasn't there." Cal's brows came down. "Clara sure looked pretty last night, but different, too. I saw her a couple of times looking all glowy and happy, but then towards the end of the evening she changed. Kinda pale and fragile. Like she was walking on eggshells and carrying fine crystal. You think she's coming down with something?"

Guilt wrapped its fist around Alec's heart. He said nothing, staring at the horizon.

Cal went on. "I couldn't get too close to her during the party, but I could see she was looking for someone most of the night. I figured it must be you. Did you two have a fight or something?"

"No, we didn't fight." Alec's words came out sharper than he'd intended. "Just leave it alone. We're out here to round up cattle, not palaver like old women." He heeled Smoke in the ribs and surged ahead of his chatty—and nosy—little brother.

They pitched camp in a glade formed by a bend in the river. Windy set up his cook fire, and several of the hands spread out to start driving cattle toward the camp. Alec and Cal built two fires out on the flat and stuck the Cross B branding irons into the flames.

The first cows showed up, driven in by the hands. A pair of cowboys circled the herd and kept them bunched, while Alec eased his horse into the animals and cut out a calf. His rope whirled once over his head. A perfect cast, the line settled over the calf's shoulders. Smoke stopped the instant the rope tugged around the saddle horn. On the ground, a cowboy flopped the calf and knelt on its neck. The smell of cows, campfires, and burning hair rose with the dust of hundreds of churning feet, and over it all, the lowing of the cows and the bawling of the calves, the shouts of the men, and Riley's bark. Controlled chaos.

Alec gathered in his rope and shook out another loop, heading back into the herd to cut out another unbranded animal. The work was demanding, but he couldn't shed the heavy, hopeless feeling in his chest.

By nightfall, Alec's muscles ached. Dust coated him from head to foot. When he stripped the saddle from Smoke's back and turned the gelding into the rope corral, his arms burned with exertion. He washed up in the creek as best he could before heading into camp.

The cook handed him a tin plate. "There's plenty more after that. Eat up."

Alec sagged onto his bedroll and dipped a biscuit in the gravy on his plate. His stomach rumbled. No self-respecting cowboy stopped for a midday meal, and breakfast in the bunkhouse that morning seemed a lifetime ago.

Riley flopped down in a cloud of dust at Alec's feet, tongue lolling. Cal plopped down on one side of Alec, and Trace folded his long frame onto his blanket on the other side. Cal balanced three biscuits on the rim of his plate, smiling broadly, ever the favored one.

Trace's eyes glittered in the light of the campfire. He dug in his pocket for the tally book. "Today's count."

Alec set his plate on the ground, wary of Riley's eager eyes on the meal, and opened the battered little book. Trace's carefully penciled columns showed up when Alec tilted the book toward the flames. He scanned the numbers then flipped back to last year's totals. "We're down some." He did a rapid calculation in his head.

Cal shook his head, mopping up gravy with a biscuit. "It's too early to say. It's only the first day. We've got a good week of fogging up these canyons and breaks yet. The numbers will come up."

Trace rolled his shoulders and shook his head. "Maybe."

The beef contracts the Colonel held loomed large in Alec's mind. He had thought the contracts a bit of a stretch with the stock they had. If he couldn't round up enough steers, they'd have to substitute breeding stock, a blow that could take years to recover from. But there was most likely an easy explanation, and as Cal said, it was mighty early to be worrying. The cows were in this canyon somewhere.

"Tomorrow, Cal, you come with me. We'll start up the canyons near Seb Lewis's boundary. Riley can bust cows out of the brush for us. Maybe the cattle have worked up farther into the draws than usual." Alec had himself convinced by the time he finished.

Cal took their empty plates to the washtub. The fire died down, and each man rolled into his blanket. An owl called softly, starting its nightly hunt. Water chuckled in the creek nearby, and a slight breeze whispered through the treetops. Alec relaxed, bit by bit, until sleep hovered a breath away.

"Alec, you asleep?" Cal nudged him.

Alec's eyes popped open. "What do you want?"

"You remember talking to Seb in the Rusty Bucket the day Clara came home?"

The familiar pain jabbed Alec's heart at the mention of her name. He cast back in his mind to coffee at the café. "Yeah, I remember."

"Think it's a coincidence that Seb's missing cows and our numbers are looking thin, too?" Cal kept his voice low.

Trace stirred next to Alec. "Seb Lewis?"

"Yeah, he told us his spring tally was way down." Cal propped himself up on his elbow.

"Did he report it to Sheriff Powers?" Trace didn't wait for an answer. "Think there's any connection with the rash of stage robberies we've had?" Alec could almost feel the frustration in Trace's voice at the law's inability to catch the band of robbers plaguing the stage line over the past couple of months. The outlaws seemed to melt away before every posse.

"I think we're getting ahead of ourselves here." Alec rolled to his side and tried to get comfortable on the hard ground. "Robbing stages and rustling cows are two different things. And anyway, we don't even know if we're missing any cattle for sure."

Though weary to the bone, sleep eluded Alec.

❧

Clara kept her hands folded in her lap, gripping her gloves. Her pale blue skirts fluttered in the breeze created by the buggy's movement. The glossy chestnut trotted briskly, eating up the miles to Steadman's property. Clara sat as still as she could, her emotions tight, as if they would all tumble into a shattered heap if she jostled them just the slightest bit.

Every thought centered on Alec. Where was he now? What was he doing? What was he thinking? Had she totally misread his intentions? Perhaps he felt nothing for her. Perhaps it was all a mistake. But no. Alec was a man of honor. He would've kissed her if his father hadn't interrupted. Alec McConnell wouldn't kiss a girl without having some feelings for her. And yet, he hadn't come to find her, hadn't been seen at the party at all, in fact. Something held him back. She felt the reserve in him, the stillness that crept over him when his father appeared. And now he was out on the range, inaccessible to her for almost a week. What would she say to him when they met again?

Steadman's house, a gracious, three-story white clapboard with gables and gingerbread trim, rose from the land like a fine lady. The former owner, a Carolinian who had escaped the war with his fortune intact—rumor had it he had done well as a blockade runner and black market dealer—had invested heavily in the house, trying to recreate his Southern plantation home.

Horses and cattle grazed in a hillside pasture, cowhands worked around the huge barn and in the corrals, the ranch bustling and busy, throwing off an air of prosperity and industry. Steadman's foreman seemed to have done well by his employer in the last year and a half since the property had changed hands.

Steadman greeted them at the front porch. In his well-tailored clothing, Clara thought he looked more like an Eastern country gentleman than a rough-and-ready ranch owner from Idaho Territory. She barely touched his hand as she stepped down.

Her father mounted the stairs, his eyes sweeping, taking in everything. "Afternoon, Devers."

"Welcome. Please, come in. I'm so glad you've come." Steadman held the door for Clara.

Her shoes echoed on the maple floor. She checked her appearance in the mirrored hall tree and adjusted a few escaping tendrils.

"Come into the parlor." He pushed open a pair of pocket doors. "I'll tell my cook you're here."

Clara was immediately transported back to some of the finest parlors of the Boston Brahmins. A large fireplace dominated the formal space. Clara ran her fingers along the curved oaken back of a velvet settee. Colorful rugs covered the floor, an extravagance and housekeeping headache in this Western land.

"Devers must have done quite well for himself to afford a place like this." The Colonel clasped his hands behind his back and stared at the still life over the mantel.

Clara settled into a chair and crossed her ankles, tucking

them back tight against the chair as she had been taught. A clock ticked somewhere in the hall.

Steadman returned. "I'm so pleased to have company. You're my first visitors." Creases appeared on either side of his mouth when he smiled, not quite dimples, but close enough to give him an appealing, almost boyish look.

Clara smiled back, remembering how he had shielded her from the stage robbers. Though a part of her mind and all her heart were centered on Alec, she roused herself to be a proper guest. "Your home is lovely."

"I'm afraid I can't take much credit for that. I bought it sight unseen through a broker in Chicago."

The Colonel took a seat on the divan. "What brought you clear out to Idaho Territory?" He propped his hand on his walking stick. "It's a long way to come for land you've never seen."

Steadman laughed, relaxed. "It sure is. I had no idea just how far. I thought I'd be on that stage forever." He glanced at Clara. "Forgive me, Miss Clara, for bringing up such a dreadful time. I understand the sheriff has not managed to apprehend those outlaws yet."

"No, they escaped capture this time."

The Colonel turned the conversation back. "So you're from Chicago then? You have family there?"

"Actually, my family hails from St. Paul. I was in Chicago on business when I met the broker selling this property. It seemed the perfect way to exercise my penchant for adventure. You see, I'm considered the wild one in my family, now that my Uncle Richard has passed on. It was because of my Uncle Richard that I wanted to get into ranching. He had a spread in East Texas, and I visited him once when I was a boy. I guess my love of wide open spaces started there. My mother nearly fainted when she heard I was moving so far west. She was glad I had to delay coming out here for so long. My father passed away suddenly just before I was going to depart, and I stayed to help settle his estate and see that she was properly cared for."

"She should come visit, see how well you've done for yourself buying this property."

"That would be something, my mother on a ranch. Ah, here's the tea. Miss Clara, would you pour, please?" Again he shone his smile full force on Clara.

"Of course." She prepared her father's tea the way he liked it—two sugars—and passed it to him. Then she looked at Steadman.

"I take it just as it is." His long, lean hand accepted the cup from her. "I can see you've fully recovered from the rigors and dangers of our journey here and the festivities of your homecoming party. You're radiant today."

The Colonel cleared his throat. "We're in your debt for what you did for Clara on the stage."

"Nonsense, whatever debt you might have owed me was more than repaid by your gracious invitation to your homecoming party. I—and my men—had a wonderful time. A chance to dance with Clara Bainbridge more than wiped out any debt." He set his cup down, not taking his eyes off her.

His bold stare made her skin prickle like she'd been out in the sun too long. It gratified her just a bit that here was a man who showed none of Alec's reluctance, but he roused in Clara none of the longing she felt when she thought of Alec. She glanced at her father.

He wore a satisfied look. "Yes, Devers, you have a lovely home here. A real showplace."

"Thank you, Colonel. All it lacks is a woman's touch. I shall have to be on the lookout for a suitable young lady. My mother says it is high time I was married." His eyes bored into Clara's.

The Colonel nodded. "Any woman you brought here would be blessed indeed. She'd be chatelaine of this fine house, the envy of the territory." He cast a not-so-subtle glance at Clara.

Clara stiffened, her cheeks heating. Steadman's expression made her feel as if he would like to slap a brand on her that very moment.

seven

Clara met the Cross B riders at the corral. The ten days since the party had dragged out for her. She'd been alone in the house for the past three days, her father having been called to the territorial capital for urgent business. With no one to talk to but herself and the woman who came in to do the washing twice a week, she'd eagerly awaited the return of the roundup crew.

Her heart lodged in her throat as they approached. Alec rode in front, as always, his familiar frame easy to pick out. Trace and Cal rode on either side.

She brought her fingers to her lips, remembering how close Alec had come to kissing her, the feel of his hands on her shoulders drawing her near. Again she wondered what might have happened if his father hadn't interrupted.

Dust flew as they trotted into the corral. Alec dismounted and reached up for a calf that lay across his saddle. The pitiful animal offered no resistance, head lolling, tongue hanging out.

Clara hurried to it, caressing its head, murmuring in its ear.

"Clara," Alec's voice sounded hoarse, strained, "bring a little warm milk to the barn. This little fellow's about done in."

Business first. Everything she wanted to say, everything she wanted to ask him, clamored inside her, but the men and horses milling around her and the sorry little calf forced her to be silent. She hurried to the kitchen and stirred up the stove. In a few minutes she raced to the barn with a kettle of slightly warmed milk and water and a handful of clean rags.

Alec knelt holding the calf's head, arranging the long, limp legs in the straw. He looked up at her and her breath caught in her throat. Several days' whiskers darkened his cheeks, and several layers of dirt and grime covered his clothes and hair. His hat bore sweat stains around the hatband, and his sleeve was ripped near the elbow. The odors of smoke and outdoors clung to him.

She swallowed and stepped into the stall. Alec scooted away. She frowned, stifling a sigh, and knelt beside the calf. Alec acted like she might bite him. Or throw herself at him.

She dipped a rag in the warm milk and squeezed it onto the calf's tongue. The animal blinked his sickle-moon lashes, a light coming into his brown eyes. "There you go, baby. You like that, don't you?"

Alec crouched against the wall, arms crossed on his knees. "How many calves have you fed this way, do you reckon?"

Clara shrugged and shook her head. "I missed this in Boston. Mama and I used to do this every spring." She smiled at him, stroking the calf's warm neck as it suckled milk from the cloth.

For a moment, Alec's mask dropped, and he smiled back like he used to. Her skin tingled and grew warm, then Alec stood up as if she'd jabbed him with a poker and stalked out of the stall. Clara blinked.

Cal scooted in, colliding with Alec in the doorway. "Hey, Clara, how's the little fella doing?" He squatted, his spurs digging into his back pockets. "Alec came across him this morning in a ravine. His mama was nowhere to be found."

"He's taking the milk." She rubbed the calf's throat to encourage him to swallow. "How'd things go on the roundup?"

Cal swept his hat off, rubbing his fingers through his sweat-plastered hair. "Not good. We rode nearly every inch of the ranch, but even with the new calves added in, the numbers are down."

"Winterkill?"

Cal's eyebrows dove inward. "Winter wasn't that bad. They're here somewhere, but I'm blamed if I know where. There's no outlet, and the only other ranch in the Money Creek basin is Seb Lewis's little place."

"Seb Lewis was talking about missing cattle at the party last week. Did you find any of his drifted onto Cross B land?" Clara dipped the cloth in the milk again. The calf shifted until he rested on his brisket, legs tucked tight, moist pink nose sniffing for food. Amazing how getting a little milk into a distressed calf could perk it up so quickly.

"A few here and there, but no more than previous years, and if I had to hazard a guess, I'd say less. The farther east and south we went, the fewer cows we found. What'd you do while we were gone?"

"We visited the Lazy P last week. Had tea with Steadman Devers."

"Hmm. And how is the new neighborhood dandy?"

"Cal, be nice. He can't help it if he's from the city. And he's doing well. The ranch looks to be in good hands. His foreman seems to know what he's doing. They were rounding up cattle, too."

"How's the calf?" Alec's voice startled them. He leaned over the stall door.

Clara's hand tightened on the rag, dribbling milk over the calf's face. "He's coming around."

"And how is the new neighbor?" Alec's brows lowered and his mouth set in a firm line.

"Fine. He has a beautiful home. I hadn't realized how grand it was. Before we left, he showed us the library and said I could borrow books any time I wanted. He's got an entire set of Shakespeare's works. Steadman's quite a reader himself. And he's interested in art. He'd been to Boston before, so it was nice to talk about places we'd both been."

"Sounds like you two had quite a chat." He frowned at her as if she'd done something wrong.

His words flicked her. "Are you implying something?"

"No, just that you sure learned a lot about him from one little visit."

Cal stood up and edged his way past Alec. "C'mon, Alec. Let's get cleaned up and go see the Colonel. Clara, don't worry about coming down to the barn tonight. I'll feed the calf."

"The Colonel isn't here. He got called away on business."

Alec's head came up. "You're here by yourself?"

"No, Jack and Pauli are here." The two pensioned-off ranch hands lived in a cabin a hundred yards behind the bunkhouse and did light work around the place. "And Bridey came in to do laundry twice. The Colonel asked me to go along with him, but I wanted to stay home."

"You shouldn't be in that big house by yourself. Anything could've happened to you. You might've gotten sick or hurt yourself somehow, and there'd be nobody to check in on you but a couple of old men. What was your father thinking?" Alec turned on his boot heel and stalked outside.

Cal followed, turning back to give Clara a low wave, his brows down, expression puzzled.

No more puzzled than Clara herself. What had gotten into Alec? He was as touchy as a bull with a bee-stung nose. She must've dreamed what happened the night of the party and only imagined he might feel something for her beyond being a protective sort of older brother.

❧

For several days, Alec managed to avoid Clara. He spent the majority of the time in the saddle, scouring the hills for pockets of cattle they might have missed during roundup.

Alec returned to the barn late one evening. Expecting the hands to have gone to bed long ago, he was surprised to see lantern light streaming from the doorway. He unsaddled and turned his mount into the corral, then picked up his gear and made for the barn.

Dread kicked him in the gut. Clara stood beside the stall at the far end of the barn. Pippa's stall. Lantern light bathed her face in a warm, golden glow. He schooled his expression and braced himself for the hammer-blow of guilt that hit every time he saw or even thought about Clara since the night of the party.

"How much longer?" She spoke to someone in the stall. Alec walked slowly down to stand beside her and leaned sideways to set his saddle down. Clara looked up into his eyes, and a delicate flush crept up her cheeks. She moistened her lips, and Alec swallowed hard.

"Can't tell." Cal's voice broke through the tension around them. He came from behind the mare who shuffled in the deep straw bedding. "She's been at it awhile but doesn't seem to be getting on with the job."

Alec's mouth went dry. For almost a month, he had kept Pippa close to the barn, expecting her to foal any day. The gentle little horse meant the world to Clara and the Colonel. Mrs. Bainbridge, the winter before she died, had talked often of a spring mating of Pippa and Champion. A year later, this foal would be the result. This morning when Alec had checked on her before he left, nothing had seemed amiss, though he had brought her inside where someone could look in on her more easily. "Have you had a feel around inside?" He took off his hat and ran his fingers through his hair.

"Not yet. I didn't want to if I didn't have to. Anyway, you're better at that kind of thing than me." Cal ran his hand along the mare's back.

She stuck her neck out flat and nickered, stamping her back foot and swishing her tail. Dark, sweaty patches marred her bright chestnut coat, and she bit at her side.

"Can't you do something for her?" Clara kept her attention on Pippa, but her hands clenched the wood in front of her. When Cal came out of the stall, she ducked in to stroke the mare's white blaze and whisper reassurances to her.

Alec blew out a long breath. "I don't like messing around in there. Apt to do more harm than good."

Cal reached up into his hatband and took out a toothpick. He clamped it between his molars and spoke around it. "Might have to take that chance. She's not overly large, and there's been no progress at all. She's getting tired out. When she strains hard, you can just see a pair of hooves, but they disappear as soon as the contraction's over." He nudged Alec and jerked his head toward Clara. "We've been watching since just before dinner. It's getting on for ten o'clock now."

Alec's mind galloped through the possibilities, none of them good. "Has she been down?"

"A few times. But she gets right back up."

Alec entered the stall and ran his hand against the mare's side. Her ribs moved like bellows, and she spraddled her legs and tensed. The muscles along her flanks tightened, and she groaned.

He made up his mind. "Get me a bucket of water and some soap."

Cal disappeared.

"What can I do?" Clara's eyes looked enormous.

"Find me some more light, and some sacking or cloths or something."

Before they returned, Alec broke open another bale and spread it in the stall. He went to his saddle and grabbed his piggin' string and tucked it into his belt. If he got this wrong, he'd never forgive himself. He snorted. Add it to his long list of sins and shortcomings.

Cal met him coming back, set the bucket he was carrying down in the aisle, and tossed Alec the soap.

Alec lathered his arm, working his sleeve well up toward his shoulder, grimacing at how tight it was. Out of deference to Clara, he wouldn't strip to the waist.

Before he'd finished, she stepped into the barn, a lantern in each hand and a pile of towels pinned under her arm.

"It's going to take all three of us. Cal, you stay at the mare's head. Clara, stay out there until I call for you." He pointed to the aisle.

Alec's initial examination confirmed his fears. He withdrew his hand and went out of the stall. "It's bad. The foal's head is laid back along its side. There's no way she can deliver like that." He took the thin rope from under his belt and dropped it into the bucket. Fishing for the bar of soap, he lathered his hands and slid the wet rope in his palm, soaping it. "I'm going to try to get a loop over the foal's jaw." He rinsed the rope. "If I can get it on, I'll need you beside me to keep it tight while I try to push the foal backwards. If you pull while I push, maybe the head will come around. All right?"

Clara nodded.

Alec knew she was aware that if this didn't work, they'd have to put Pippa down. Better to be mercifully quick than for the mare to die a slow, agonizing death. The thought of Clara's tear-filled and reproachful eyes seared him. Not to mention how the news might hit the Colonel.

As Alec stepped into the stall, Pippa went down onto the straw. He motioned for Clara to come in. "Cal, keep her down." Alec stretched out behind the mare and tucked the rope between his first two fingers.

Clara knelt in the straw beside him, holding the mare's tail out of the way and staying clear of Pippa's rear hooves, lest she thrash about. A powerful contraction rippled through the mare and squeezed Alec's arm until his fingers went numb. Cal kept up a constant stream of murmurs into the mare's ear, though Alec couldn't make out what his youngest brother was saying. He glanced up at Clara's pale face. Her lips moved in what he assumed was a silent prayer.

He sent up a prayer of his own. *Help me, Lord. I know the foal's most likely dead, probably strangled awhile ago, but if You could save the mare. . .*

The foal's muzzle lay just inches beyond the farthest point Alec could reach. He even pulled on one slick ear, trying to get the little head around, but he couldn't get a good enough purchase, and his fingers slipped. Each contraction crushed his arm against the mare's bony pelvis. Finally, knowing he had to make this happen soon or admit defeat, he jammed his boots hard against the corner of the stall and braced himself for one last effort. Stretching to the fullest, he brushed the foal's lower jaw. His arm shook, and his shoulder muscles screamed, but he managed to slip the rope on.

"Clara, grab this line." He rocked to his side to give her room, praying the rope wouldn't slip off. Once she had the line taut, he withdrew until he could push the palm of his hand against the foal's chest. "Pull, Clara, nice and steady." Sweat dripped into Alec's face and stung his eyes. The foal's head came around to lie on the long forelegs. Alec relaxed and withdrew his hand all the way.

As if Pippa now knew things were right, she gave a weak heave. The rope slipped off the foal, and Clara tipped over on Alec. He grunted as the wind went out of him.

"Is that it? Did we do it?" Clara scrambled up, elbowing him in the stomach in her haste.

Alec rubbed his middle and nodded. When he could speak,

he gasped, "The mare's tired out. We better help her."

He wrapped his hands around the protruding hooves, and when the next contraction hit, he tugged gently. Slippery, slab-sided, and limp, the foal slid from the mare and plopped onto the straw. No signs of life. Though he'd expected it, disappointment still shot through him.

"It's a filly." Clara tucked her laced fingers under her chin.

"I'm sorry, Clara." The foal had been too long in the birthing canal. It was bound to be dead. But at least they'd saved the mare.

Cal released Pippa's head, but she was so exhausted, she didn't get up. Clara reached for a towel while Alec propped himself against the side of the stall and hung his wrists on his updrawn knees. At her exclamation, his head came up.

The foal's legs twitched. The bony rib cage jerked and settled into a steady rise-and-fall rhythm. Clara snatched up a towel and wiped the little muzzle. The dark eyes, fringed with long, wet, spiky lashes fluttered open. "She's alive." Clara breathed the words and turned her joy-filled face toward Alec.

New life shot through his tired muscles. *Thank You, Lord.*

Cal reached down his hand to help Alec rise. "Looks a lot like Pippa."

Clara wiped the white blaze on the little chestnut face. "She does." Something in her voice drew Alec's attention. She whispered, "Mama would've liked that."

Alec sluiced his arm with water from the bucket and scrubbed it dry with one of the towels. Mrs. Bainbridge *would've* liked this little filly. Hard to believe Clara's mother had been gone a whole year. He owed her so much. Even more than he owed the Colonel, truth be told. He shoved down those thoughts.

"Let's introduce these two." Alec gathered the foal up and carried her around to the mare's head.

Pippa whickered and nuzzled the baby, her liquid eyes brightening as she *whuffed* along the filly's neck. The mare rolled onto her chest and gathered her legs under her. She lurched up while Alec held the foal to make sure she didn't get stepped on. When Pippa lowered her head to lick the wet newborn, Alec laid her down and joined Cal and Clara in the stall doorway. Within minutes, the foal tried to stand and before long had found her way to her feet and along Pippa's flank to nurse.

Alec tried to ignore how right it felt to stand here beside Clara, sharing this special moment.

"God sure is amazing." Cal shoved his hat back on his head. "It's a miracle, no matter how many times you see it."

The rattle of a buggy and horses' hooves broke the silence. The Colonel strode down the aisle. "Clara, I thought you'd be in bed long since."

"Look, Father, Pippa's foaled. It's a filly." She took his hand and drew him to the stall.

Cal stepped back and waved Alec away when he headed toward the buggy. "I'll unhitch the team."

The Colonel stroked his moustache, moisture gathering in his eyes as he stared at the foal, saying nothing. Clara kept hold of his hand. "I miss her, too."

Alec picked up his saddle to put it away, allowing father and daughter some privacy. The light from the aisle barely reached the tack room, but he didn't need it. The sheepskin-covered saddle rack by the door had his name on the end. He settled the saddle-tree onto the rack and draped his bridle on the horn, ready for the morning.

When he returned to Clara's side, she had tears on her cheeks. The Colonel handed her a handkerchief.

"What are you going to call her?" Alec blew out one of the lanterns.

"She's a little bit of a thing, and Mama would've loved her. I think we should call her Bitsy." Clara wiped her cheeks and looked to her father, her eyebrows raised.

Alec froze. Bitsy. He hadn't heard that name in over a year. The Colonel had called his wife, Elizabeth Bainbridge, Bitsy.

The Colonel's jaw tightened then relaxed. "Then Bitsy it is."

eight

Clara placed her hand in her father's and stepped from the wagon onto Money Creek's main street. She surveyed Purdy's Mercantile from the false-front upper story to the ground floor windows laden with everything from guns to gumdrops. The sight did nothing to soothe feelings, ruffled from arguing with her father on the trip to town.

"I don't want you wandering around town alone. Alec will help you with your trading and carry your parcels." Father consulted his pocket watch. "We'll meet at the Rusty Bucket just before noon, and I'll treat you to lunch."

Clara closed her eyes and prayed for patience. "Alec doesn't need to stay with me. I'm perfectly capable of doing the shopping on my own. He surely has better things to do than traipse after me while I look at dress goods." She glanced up at Alec, who shifted his weight from one foot to the other, staring at the boardwalk, giving her no help at all.

"Clara, we've been all through this. The town's changed some since you've been away. Mineral strikes close to town mean all kinds of men are pouring into the area. I'd rather be safe than sorry, so you need an escort. I can't take on that duty at the moment; I have to meet with a couple of investors in the new branch stage line." He turned to Alec. "Don't let her out of your sight."

Alec nodded and hooked his thumbs through his belt loops. His eyes scanned the street, his expression wary. He looked for all the world like a payroll guard expecting a robbery attempt. He'd maintained the same stoic expression all the way into town, brooding and remote.

Clara resigned herself to a keeper. What once would've been a treat, a day in town with Alec, now chafed when her father put him in the role of minder. The ease with which Clara and Alec had worked together to deliver Pippa's foal had disappeared the instant they stepped out of the barn that night. He went back to holding her at arm's length, relegating her to the role of a stranger he must be polite to.

She squared her shoulders and stepped to the entrance. "Let's go. I have a lot to accomplish if I'm to be done by noon."

Alec held the door for her, and the bell on the lintel jangled cheerily. He looked like a man condemned and walking to his own hanging.

Clara sighed. Armed with her list of purchases to be made, she entered the store. A hundred different sights and smells wrapped around her ranging from the luster of the shiny saddle on a sheepskin rack by the door to the dusty smell of flour from a barrel. Twin counters ran the length of the store, piled with goods. She passed the oat bins and pickle barrel, wrinkling her nose at the sharp brine, and consulted her list.

Mrs. Purdy, a tiny woman with jet black hair and eyes, stomped over.

Clara hid her grin. Folks of Money Creek had long joked that Mrs. Purdy walked like she was carrying a grand piano on her back. Though she couldn't weigh much more than a hundred pounds, her footsteps sounded like an advancing infantry on the store's floorboards.

"Why, Clara Bainbridge, if you aren't a sight for sore eyes. Welcome home, dear. I'm so sorry I couldn't make it to the party. Mr. Purdy"—she leaned close, eyes sparkling—"well, he gets a touch bilious every now and again. I had to stay and tend to him."

"I'm sorry to hear that. I hope he is feeling better soon."

Clara smoothed the paper in her hand and set it on the counter.

"Oh, never you fear. I had him back on his feet in no time. Fixed him up with my secret medicine, I did." Her hand flitted like a bird's wing toward the pharmacy area. "I'm thinking I should bottle some up and sell it here in the store. It's a miracle drug. The trick is to put in enough asafetida to work but not upset the digestion." She looked over Clara's shoulder and sucked in a breath so hard that for an instant her bottom lip disappeared. Her eyes glowed like rivets fresh out of the blacksmith's forge.

Alec's hands fisted, and he braced his legs apart as if expecting trouble. When he glanced at Clara, he relaxed a fraction and touched the brim of his hat. "Mrs. Purdy." He folded his arms across his chest.

"Alec is helping me today, Mrs. Purdy." Clara turned to Alec. "I'm going to be quite a while. You don't have to stay."

"Colonel's orders. I'm staying." His mouth tightened. "I won't touch anything, Mrs. Purdy. I'm just here to fetch and carry for Clara. I'll stay right here by the door."

Clara stifled a sigh. For a moment she'd forgotten the grudge Mrs. Purdy had against Alec. It appeared that nothing had changed in over a year. Poor Alec. Forever dogged by his past. How long would it be before Mrs. Purdy forgave him his mistake? Couldn't she see the change that had come over Alec? He might have stolen from her once, more than three years ago, but he'd paid it back and hadn't touched a thing that belonged to someone else since.

"Well, it's stuffy in here. Open the door." Mrs. Purdy sniffed down her sharp little nose and consulted Clara's list. Her glance returned often to Alec, but she said no more.

He obliged, swinging the door wide to let in whatever fresh air might dare to wander near.

Clara turned toward the counter. "I'd like to see some summer-weight calico, if I may. Something in blue would be nice." Alec's favorite color. He'd once told her it made her eyes prettier than a summer sky when she wore blue.

Mrs. Purdy lifted down two bolts of cloth. "That dress you're wearing is so stylish. Is that the newest fashion? You'll have to tell me all about Boston. Sometimes I despair of bringing any progress to this frontier town. All folks seem to want is calicos and denim. Let me show you this." She tugged a lavender bolt from the bottom of a stack on the shelf above her head. "I've had this voile for three years and haven't sold so much as a yard. Isn't that a shame? I suppose it is impractical for every day, but you'd think at least one woman out here would buy it to make a church dress."

Clara fingered the delicate cloth. "It is lovely. Perhaps you should make it up for yourself. Ladies might be more inclined to buy it if they saw you wearing it." Again Clara hid a smile. Somehow the image of the indomitable Mrs. Purdy stalking down the street toward the church, shoulders thrown back, Bible tucked under her arm like a riding crop, lavender voile wafting in her wake, made Clara want to giggle.

Mrs. Purdy snorted and shook her head. She wore matronly black every day, summer and winter, without exception. That bolt of cloth was destined to languish on the shelf.

Clara worked her way down her dry-goods list then started on the groceries. Alec remained by the open door, arms crossed, face a mask of indifference.

While Mrs. Purdy jotted notes, two male voices filtered in from the boardwalk. "I'm telling you, there's something going on. Seb Lewis told me he's short by a bunch. When he took the news to the sheriff, you know what Powers said? Said plain as day he thought it was the McConnell boys. And it makes sense. Who else could sneak cows out of Money

Creek Canyon right under the old man's nose? You know what they say, once a thief, always a thief. You know every last one of those McConnell boys have been in Powers's jail at one time or another."

"That might be, but I'd keep my trap shut if I was you. One of those boys might get wind you're talking about them and stop by your place for a little chat. They might be shifty, but I wouldn't want to cross one of them. Every one of them can hit hard enough to drop an ox, and they're no slouches when it comes to shooting either."

Clara turned from the counter. How dare they? She stalked toward the door and stepped into the sunshine. "Excuse me, I couldn't help but overhear your conversation." She kept her voice low, trying to control the anger rising within her at the injustice of their comments. "I don't know the problem to which you were referring, but I can assure you, none of the McConnell boys had anything to do with it."

"Don't, Clara."

"But they were saying—" She looked over her shoulder to find Alec right behind her.

His brown eyes shot hot daggers through the two men. "I heard them. You don't have to defend the McConnells to a pair like this. It won't do any good anyway. People have long memories, and they're not quick to forgive. We could act like saints for a month of Sundays and it wouldn't matter. Money Creek believes what it wants to believe, lies or not."

Clara shivered at his icy tone.

The two men crowded together, shoulder-to-shoulder. "You calling us liars?" The shorter of the two sneered at Alec.

Alec's hands clamped around Clara's upper arms, and he pushed her behind him. "If you're saying I stole cattle from Seb Lewis or Colonel Bainbridge, then yes, you are a liar."

Thwack!

Everyone jumped.

Mrs. Purdy raised the yardstick and poised to strike it on the doorjamb again. "There's no fighting in or around my store. You scoundrels get out, or I'll send for the sheriff."

The two men backed away from the feisty little woman. They looked from her to Alec and back again, as if trying to assess the greater threat. One bumped into the hitching rail in his haste to escape.

Alec relaxed his stance and turned to go back into the store.

Mrs. Purdy stopped him with the yardstick in his chest. "You'll stay out here, McConnell."

Alec stared at the woman for a long moment then removed his hat to run his fingers through his hair. He resettled his Stetson and touched the brim. "Ma'am." He turned to Clara. "Let me know when you're finished." Straight-backed and proud, he stepped onto the dusty street and leaned against the hitching rail where he could see into the store.

Clara roused herself from her surprised shock and turned to Mrs. Purdy. Anger at the injustice of the storekeeper's actions flared, making her skin feel hot. She snatched her shopping list from the woman's hand. "I don't believe I'll be buying anything from you today. Cancel my order, Mrs. Purdy. I'll do my trading elsewhere." Chin high, she joined Alec on the road.

❧

Embarrassment and anger tightened the muscles of Alec's neck and shoulders. His hands clenched and unclenched, itching to hit something just to relieve his feelings.

"Of all the uncalled for, unnecessary, un-Christian things to do, that takes the biscuit." Clara fumed by his side. "She had no right to treat you that way."

"Stop fussing. It won't change anything." They headed up

the board sidewalk toward the café.

"When are people going to stop treating you like a pariah? It's ridiculous. Anyone with two eyes could see you're not the same as you used to be."

Alec shrugged. "I'm used to it." He wasn't, but he liked to pretend he was.

"Well, I'm not. I knew you had a history with some of the shopkeepers, and with Sheriff Powers, but I thought it would all die down. It's been over three years, hasn't it?"

"Three years this past spring. But like I said, folks have long memories for some things. Pa's a constant reminder, too, that McConnells are no good. And if the town manages to forget for a spell, the sheriff brings it up again." Alec took her elbow to cross the street. "You might be sorry you locked horns with Mrs. Purdy. She won't be quick to forgive that slight."

He held the door for her and swept off his hat before entering the café. Clara's flying to his defense pleased him, but it hurt, too. He reminded himself once more that this was why he had to stay away from her, had to guard his feelings from her. If he ever courted her, he would be dooming her to a life of having to defend them both. He wouldn't expose her to the ridicule he faced nearly every time he went to town.

With a practiced flip, he tossed his hat onto a peg by the entrance. The restaurant was half filled with people. Georgia seemed to fill the other half, her red hair like a bonfire signaling her presence.

Clara wended her way through the tables to where her father sat. He rose in greeting, as did his companion. Alec stifled a groan. That greenhorn rancher, Devers.

Alec gritted his teeth when Devers stood and took Clara's hand. "Ah, the day is brightened. You look lovely, Clara." He held out the chair next to him for her to be seated. "Have you been shopping?"

Alec slid back a chair for himself. He flopped down, feeling mulish. A whole day wasted in town when he should be back at the Cross B looking for stray cattle. And now he had to endure the presence of Steadman "Upper-Crust" Devers.

Clara didn't seem to mind the attention. She smiled at Devers in a way that made Alec's stomach churn. "I have been shopping, but the morning wasn't very successful. I didn't find anything I needed at Purdy's. I'll have to try Goddard's after lunch."

The Colonel frowned. "We've always traded at Purdy's. What is it you were looking for that you couldn't find there?"

Alec studied his hands, hoping Clara wouldn't go into any details. But Clara was in a full gallop of indignation. Easier to stop a blizzard wind. Clara answered, her palms pressed on the table. "I was looking for some respect. I had a rather unpleasant encounter with Mrs. Purdy over some unruly loiterers."

"Alec, where were you? You didn't let some ruffian accost Clara? That's why I sent you along with her." The Colonel's voice rose with his agitation.

Alec straightened in his chair, but Clara intervened before he could say anything. "No, Father, it was nothing like that. Don't worry yourself. Alec was a perfect gentleman and looked after me very well. I just don't choose to return to Purdy's. Goddard's will be fine."

Georgia slapped coffee cups on the table for Alec and Clara and plucked the pencil from behind her ear. "What'll it be, folks?" She seemed to focus on who they were for the first time and her manner softened. "Hello, Alec. You expecting Cal to join you? Lily made bread pudding, and I know how he loves bread pudding."

Alec shook his head, rubbing his upper lip to conceal his smile at her eagerness. "Sorry, Georgia. He didn't make the trip with us today."

Her brusque manner returned so fast it made Alec blink. "You eatin' then?" She glared at the center of the table. She bustled off with their orders, wedging herself between the tables and setting the doors into the kitchen to flopping.

"Interesting woman." Devers tucked his index fingers into his waistcoat pockets and leaned back. "But getting back to your proposal, Colonel, I agree with you that a stage line between Money Creek and Boise would be helpful to the town. However, I'm concerned about the current rash of robberies taking place south of here. If I should invest in the new line, I'd want some assurance that the cargo and passengers would be safe from bandits."

"Only a matter of time before those outlaws are apprehended." The Colonel smoothed his moustache. "Powers will track them down. Outlaws get careless eventually."

Alec toyed with his fork and glanced at the clock by the door. Daylight wasting and him here stuck listening to Steadman Devers talk about investments. This day couldn't get much worse.

"Son, might I have a word with you?"

Alec clamped his jaw tight and turned to look into the pale, watery eyes of his parent.

Correction. The day *could* get worse.

Angus shifted from foot to foot, twisting his battered hat in his gnarled hands. His cheeks shone red as if chapped by a cold wind, though it must be all of eighty degrees outside. At least he wore clean clothes and looked as if he had bathed in the last month.

"What do you want?" Alec was more than familiar with this stage of his father's behavior. He resigned himself for what was coming.

Angus rubbed his nose, cleared his throat, and nodded to those around the table. "Pardon the interruption. Just wanted to tell my son how sorry I am for the way I've been acting. But that's all behind me now. I got my job back at the livery stable, and I'm steering clear of the liquor. You'll see. Things are going to be different now." He rubbed his nose again. His eyes implored Alec to believe him this time.

Alec looked away. Not a thing was different. Angus McConnell never changed. He'd stay sober for a week, maybe even a month, but no longer. He was a slave to the bottle and always would be, and his promises meant nothing, not to a son who had heard them over and over for nearly as long as he could remember. Unless or until he let God change him, he'd stay exactly the way he was.

Georgia hustled out balancing plates of food. She thunked them down on the table, the aroma of steak and potatoes rising around them.

Alec glanced at his father. A light had come into Angus's eyes, and he licked his lips. In spite of himself, Alec asked, "When was the last time you ate?"

Angus shook his head, wiping his hand on his thigh. "I'm getting along all right. Don't worry about me."

But Alec couldn't enjoy his food if he knew his father walked away hungry. "Here, take mine. I'm not hungry anyway." He stood and handed the plate to Angus. "Go over there and eat."

Angus took the plate as if it might break in his hands. He licked his lips again and swallowed. "It will be different this time, Alec. I promise."

"Yeah." Alec turned to the Colonel. "I'll meet you at the wagon." He snagged his hat on the way out, eager to put some distance between himself and his family troubles.

nine

The foal swept under her mother's belly and ducked around her flank to peek at Clara through the mare's long, glossy tail. Clara laughed at the baby.

"Two weeks old already. About time for these two to be taken to the high pasture for the summer." Alec coiled a rope and hung it on a peg. "I'll check on how the other mares and foals are doing and bring down some of the colts to start breaking them."

The neutral tone he maintained since the foal's birth irked her. He was so detached and cool, Clara wanted to scream. She wanted to crack that icy exterior and batter down the walls he'd thrown up between them. "Can I come, too? I'd love to see the babies. It's been such a long time."

Alec tucked his hands into his back pockets. "I'm leaving in a few minutes."

Such joy filled her as they mounted, Clara wanted to throw her arms wide and take in the sunshine, the wildflowers popping up everywhere, the piney smell of the trees. Her spirit awakened as she and Alec rode side by side along Money Creek. "Now I feel as if I've really come home." She scanned the rim of the canyon.

Alec wrapped the mare's lead rope around his saddle horn. His hat brim shaded his face, but Clara could feel him looking at her. Her skin prickled with awareness.

"It was mighty quiet around here while you were gone."

The mare whickered to her foal, who had gotten too far away. The filly bucked a little and headed back to the safety of her mama's side. A mile from the house, they came to a secluded little glade ringed by pines and a few aspens. Mama's favorite spot on the ranch. A single white headstone stood in the center of the clearing. Clara pulled Hawkwing up.

Alec stopped his horse. "Let's rest for a bit. The foal needs a breather."

Clara dismounted and let her reins trail. She walked through the high grass, gathering a few wildflowers as she went. When she reached the headstone, she sank down beside it. She traced the words with her gloved fingertips.

Elizabeth Mary Bainbridge, Beloved Wife and Mother, b.1847, d.1882

Alec squatted not far away, reins in his hand, expression somber.

"She married my father when she was seventeen, did you know that? He was career army and thought he'd never marry, but when he met Mama, everything changed." Clara spread her bundle of wildflowers across the grave. "And she had me on their first anniversary. In Kansas, just after the war. But I don't remember Kansas at all. They traveled here when I was very small. Who takes care of her grave?"

"We all do, I guess. Me and Cal and Trace, and the Colonel, too. I see him ride up here sometimes."

"She thought a lot of you boys." Clara pushed her hat off, letting it hang by the stampede strap down her back. The sun warmed the crown of her head. A slight breeze teased the wisps of hair that came out of her braid.

"We owe her a lot. Without her and the Colonel, we'd probably all be in the territorial prison," Alec said.

"Your life sure would've been different if you hadn't stolen her purse, huh?" Clara remembered the belligerent young men lined up behind the bars in the jail. She'd been an awkward almost-fifteen, uneasy at Sheriff Powers storming back and forth, trying to talk Mama into pressing charges.

"The worst and best decision of my life. I don't even know why I did it. I'd stolen something from nearly every shopkeeper in Money Creek at one time or another, but I'd never taken a lady's purse before." Alec tipped his head to the side, staring somewhere far away, clearly remembering. "Powers threw us all in jail so fast the hinges on the cell door smoked. And he'd have thrown away the key, too. I was cussing him hard when your mama walked in. When she looked at me, I nearly swallowed my tongue."

Clara stayed still, not wanting to disrupt his reverie. Though she knew the story by heart, she loved to hear it again.

"That's when I first saw you, too. All eyes and long, brown braids."

She made a small noise of assent in her throat, remembering her first glimpse of the McConnell boys, shaggy hair, rough clothes in need of mending, and a wildness that both drew and repelled her.

Alec picked some grass and tossed it into the breeze. "I don't know what your mama saw in us, but her bringing us here to the ranch was a blessing." A smile tugged his mouth. "Though I doubt the Colonel thought so at first. He had to ride us pretty hard. And he didn't make any headway with us for a while. Not until Mrs. Bainbridge got through to us. And you did, too."

"Not until God got through to you."

"Yeah, but the Bainbridge women showed us the way. We were all mighty suspicious, but you kept on being kind to us. It had been a long time since a woman had been kind to us. Kinda brought back thoughts of our own mama and baby sister."

Frustration boiled up inside Clara. She wasn't his sister,

and she didn't want him to think of her as such. She turned back to the headstone.

She pulled a vine away from the base of the stone, but when she couldn't uproot it, she dug in her pocket, withdrawing a small knife and flicking open the blade.

"You still have that?" Alec motioned to the knife.

She nodded, slicing the vine and snapping the blade shut. She turned it in her palm, the bone handle worn white and smooth. "I never go anywhere without it. It was one of the best birthday gifts I ever got, mostly because I knew how much it meant to you."

Alec shrugged and stared at the treetops across the glen. "It was about the only thing I owned at the time that was really mine, bought and paid for. I'm surprised you kept it."

Clara returned the knife to her pocket. "It's been all the way to Boston and back." She brushed her fingers across the carved letters on the headstone once more.

He rose and scanned the sky, his leather chaps creaking, spurs jingling. "Let's get going if you're finished here. The foal's rested up."

☙

All the way to the horse pasture, Alec kept watch for cow sign. He'd found no strangers on the property, no sign of predator trouble, and no miraculous staircase up the canyon wall by which the cattle could walk out. But little by little, the Cross B herd was dwindling.

Alec pulled his horse up and scanned the meadow. Knee-high grass waved in the wind. A hawk circled lazily overhead, riding the air currents, looking for a meal. A deer with a pair of fawns grazed near the edge of the pasture. She raised her head, grass hanging from her mouth, to stare at the intruders.

Several mares cropped grass, their foals napping or nursing. Alec frowned and turned to look toward the creek below.

The mares lifted their heads, tails swishing, then returned to grazing. But where were the young horses, the yearlings and two-year-olds? Unease galloped up his spine.

"Wait here. And hold this." He passed the lead rope to Clara and legged Smoke into a trot. The deer's tail went up, and she bounded into the trees, her fawns spotted streaks at her heels. Alec searched the ground on either side of his horse. He circled the broad basin, trying to see into the dense undergrowth beyond for signs of the rest of the Cross B herd. He pulled up next to Clara.

The wind ruffled her collar and blew a lock of hair across her cheek. She hooked it with her little finger and tucked it behind her ear. "What is it?"

"I don't know. The mares are all here, and the foals, but the rest of the colts and fillies are gone."

"Maybe they worked their way down to the creek and decided to stay."

"We'll head that way, but I doubt it. The lead mare, Sandy, she likes this meadow, and she keeps the rest of the horses pretty much together." He unhooked his canteen, pulled the stopper, and handed it to Clara. She pressed the opening to her lips and tilted her head back. Alec looked away, his heart rate picking up.

Stop it, old son. If you let your head go that way, you'll do or say something stupid.

She handed him back the canteen, and he strapped it to his saddle once more. "We might as well turn Pippa and her foal loose. Then we can look for the rest of them lower down." He reached over and unbuckled the halter, slipping it from the mare's head. Pippa stood still for a moment, then, realizing she was free, sauntered through the grass toward the other mares, her baby at her flank.

Alec and Clara rode down the hillside toward the creek a

half mile away. When they reached the flat, they stopped to rest.

Alec swept off his hat and wiped his brow with his forearm. "How are you holding out?"

"Me? I'm fine." She looked at him accusingly. "I am capable of riding more than a few miles, no matter what my father thinks."

Alec grinned and held up his hands in surrender. "Don't get out your claws. Thought you might be getting a little tired. You took your dinners off the mantel for a few days after you rode astride the day you got home."

She ducked her chin, a smile teasing her lips. "They made us ride sidesaddle in Boston."

A shout drifted toward them. "Hello there!"

Alec turned in the saddle to look north along the creek. Two riders approached at a trot. He recognized the one in the lead immediately. A scowl curled his lip before he could control it. Steadman Devers.

His foreman, Sparks, rode behind Devers, looking as if he'd been born in the saddle, while Devers bounced and slid around, using his reins as handles and, of all things, holding one rein in each hand. They pulled to a stop close by.

Devers tipped his hat and bowed in the saddle. "Miss Clara, how fortuitous to meet you here. You're looking quite lovely today."

Alec shook his head at the fancy wording. Why couldn't this fellow just say what he wanted to say plain, without all the frills and dressings? Acted like he'd swallowed a dictionary. "You're a long way from home. What brings you to the Cross B?"

"Actually, we're headed to the Double Box to see Seb Lewis." Devers peeled off his gloves. "He's got a couple of horses for sale that I'm interested in. Sparks tells me you can never have too many good mounts on a ranch."

Sparks leaned over in the saddle and spit on the ground. His small eyes, shielded by his lowered hat brim, swept the area. "Never pass up a good horse, that's my feeling."

"How'd your herd winter?" Alec glanced at the canyon rim as if the answer didn't interest him.

Sparks shrugged. "Fair enough, I guess." His tone made it clear he wouldn't reveal more, but Devers had no reservations.

"We—or rather my hands—spent the week branding Lazy P cattle. It was all very exciting. I've never seen a roundup before."

"Did you have a good tally?"

"Sparks tells me we've held our own." Devers beamed, baring a lot of white teeth. "Clara, I do hope you'll grace my home with your presence again soon. I had such a delightful time at your last visit." The bounder actually reached over and patted Clara's hand where it rested on her saddle horn.

Alec's blood heated and charged along his veins.

"Actually, I was going to send an invitation to you to visit the Cross B. I'm having a dinner party for my father's birthday this weekend. I do hope you can come. And Mr. Sparks, too, of course." She inclined her head to the cowboy.

"We'd be delighted." Devers patted her hand again.

Alec's grip tightened on the reins, and he shifted, his saddle creaking.

"Saturday for dinner then?" Clara sent him a wide smile that made Alec's guts churn.

Before Devers could answer, Alec butted in. "We'd best get moving. I can't spend all day chewing the fat. Some of us have work to do." Alec lifted his reins and kneed Smoke into a walk back along the creek in the direction of the ranch house. "Come on, Clara."

Clara waited until they were out of earshot then turned to Alec. "You could've been a little nicer back there."

Alec grunted.

"And don't go all silent and stoic on me. You know you were rude. What have you got against Steadman Devers?"

He shrugged. "Nothing, I guess." *How about the way he looks at you, like you were the last flapjack on the plate? How about the way he marches into Money Creek and suddenly everybody's his friend? Even the Colonel likes him.*

His conscience pricked him. It was childish to be jealous, especially regarding the Colonel, who had been nothing but generous where Alec and his brothers were concerned. He should be happy that someone had come along who matched Clara in social standing, someone the Colonel liked and approved of.

But he wasn't.

Alec dragged his thoughts back to the matter at hand—missing cattle and now missing horses. He'd have to tell the Colonel soon. Alec had been putting off the meeting with the Colonel, hoping to find the missing stock or the reason behind the disappearance. But he was running out of places to search. Alec gritted his teeth. He couldn't fail the Colonel. He had to get to the bottom of things.

"Alec, let's explore Skull Canyon." Clara pointed to the opening of the maze of canyons. The buffalo skull rock from which the canyon drew its name stared down with empty sockets.

"You know better than that. Your father has it fenced off, and his orders are clear."

"There's a gate in that fence, and you know it." She shot him a disgruntled look. "But someday I'm going to find it."

"Find what?"

"A way through. Mother knew it was there somewhere."

"Your mother thought she knew, and it got her into more trouble than she could get out of. You know how dangerous it is in there. Your horse puts one foot wrong and you'll bring down an avalanche. The cliff sides are rotten. It's too dangerous, so forget any notions you have about going in there alone."

"But I wouldn't be alone." She gave him an innocent, wide-eyed stare. "You'd be with me."

"If your father found out I'd taken you in there, he'd chase me right out of Idaho Territory." He looked away from her face so he could concentrate. "Let's get home. Work's waiting."

She muttered something under her breath, but he didn't ask her what it was. He probably didn't want to know.

ten

The Colonel's birthday dinner went off without a hitch. Until dessert.

Alec couldn't help but notice the way Clara's eyes glowed in the light of the candles on the cake she carried in from the kitchen. The bell sleeves of her yellow dress fell back revealing her slender wrists.

He snatched his napkin from his lap and stood—a fraction of a second after Steadman Devers.

The light from the fancy table candles ran in silky lines along Clara's hair, and when she bent to set the cake on the table, a light floral scent accompanied the movement. "Happy birthday, Father." She smiled, her cheeks pink.

The Colonel beamed with pleasure. "Thank you, my dear. And thank all of you for coming." He looked around the table at his guests, his attention and smile lingering longest on his daughter and Devers. "I don't know if I can get all the candles blown out in one go, but I'll try."

Clara served the Colonel first then gave a big piece to Devers.

"Thank you, Miss Clara. I do wish Sparks could've joined us tonight. He sends his regrets. I know he has a particular fondness for sweets. He will be sorry to have missed this delightful treat prepared by your own fair hands."

Alec resisted rolling his eyes. Devers might as well set his comments to music he was so poetic. And Clara didn't seem to mind, not with the way she kept looking at him from under her lashes like Devers was the most fascinating man this side of Chicago.

Alec's fingers brushed Clara's as she handed him his slice of cake. Like a lightning bolt, heat shot up his arm.

She looked so beautiful tonight. The perfect hostess. He could imagine her in the finest drawing rooms of Boston, sipping tea, discussing whatever it is that women talk about.

He shifted in his seat, drawing his boots under his chair and staring at his fists. Beat up, nicked, tanned—nothing like Devers's white, smooth hands.

The Eastern dandy took a small bite then wiped his lips with his napkin. "Alec, I meant to tell you, Sparks and I did manage to acquire those two horses from Seb Lewis. His place is in a bit of disarray, though it may be unkind of me to say so. He's not exactly thriving back there on his little patch, is he? I felt compelled not to haggle over the price of the horses too much."

Trace caught Alec's eye. Last night they'd argued—a rare thing with Trace—about telling the Colonel the Cross B was headed the same direction as Lewis's Double Box if they didn't find those stray cows soon.

Hot prickles skittered across Alec's chest. He knew he should've told the Colonel the minute he suspected something amiss, but he'd hoped to be proven wrong or to be able to fix the problem before the Colonel had to find out. But he'd failed.

As if reading Alec's mind, the Colonel sat back in his chair and toyed with his fork. "Alec, you haven't gotten around to showing me the figures from our roundup." The Colonel's mild accusation stung. "I've been waiting to see how our numbers compared with those of last year."

"No, sir, I haven't reported to you just yet." Alec straightened his spine and looked his employer in the eye. "The numbers are down from last fall. By quite a bit. I should've told you right away, but I was hoping the cattle would turn up."

"I see." The Colonel pursed his lips.

Alec wanted to rub his chest to ease the unsettled feeling there, but he sat still under his employer's scrutiny.

"Any idea where the animals have gone?"

If he had an idea where they'd gone, he wouldn't be in this trouble. No, that wasn't true. If he'd come clean with the Colonel the instant he suspected they were missing cattle, he wouldn't be in this trouble. Why hadn't he?

Pride, pure and simple.

He didn't want to admit he needed the Colonel's help. He'd wanted to prove himself, to attempt to repay some of the debt he owed this man for helping him change his life. In trying to pay back the debt, he'd actually dug himself in deeper.

The silence stretched on way too long, until Cal nudged Alec's side.

Alec balled his fists. "No, sir, it's a puzzle. We've scoured the range for Cross B cows, but nothing's turned up." Alec loosened his fingers and wiped his palms on his thighs. "Sir, there's more. We're also missing about twenty head of horses. All the young stock from the high pasture." It galled Alec to have to admit all this in front of Steadman Devers, but he wouldn't evade the truth any longer. "And we don't have a clue where they've gone."

Silence hung heavy in the room. Finally, Devers cleared his throat. "Clara, it's been a delightful evening, but I fear I must take my leave. There's a good full moon tonight to guide me on the way home, but I don't want to arrive there too late." He rose and bowed at the waist. "Colonel, thank you for your hospitality." He waved Clara back when she started to rise. "No, no, my dear. You all obviously have plenty to discuss that is best talked over without a stranger in your midst. I can see myself out. Good night, gentlemen, Clara." His glossy black boots tapped on the hardwood floor, and after a moment, the front door closed behind him.

Alec didn't want to admit that Devers showed himself a decent guy by bowing out at that moment.

The Colonel spoke first. "Alec, I can't begin to understand why you'd keep this information from me. I've been waiting for weeks for you to come to me. I may be getting old"—he chuckled, his eyes kind—"but I'm not quite in my dotage yet. I've watched you ride yourself to a frazzle since the roundup. I concluded that you must be searching for something, and cattle seemed the logical thing."

His words hit Alec like a punch in the gut. All this time the Colonel had known? "Why didn't you say something?"

"I suspected you had your reasons for keeping the news from me. Not, I'll confess, the same reasons as Sheriff Powers implied when we talked it over in his office. He seemed sure that any cattle missing from Seb Lewis or the Cross B had to be an inside job. It didn't take much reasoning out that he thought you boys might be behind it."

An inside job. It didn't take a genius to realize that as the foreman of the ranch he'd be the first on the list of suspects. Alec McConnell, one of the thieving, no-good McConnells.

In his haste to stand, he toppled his chair. He tossed the fancy napkin onto his plate. "Sir, there are cattle missing, and you're right, I didn't tell you about it when I should have. I thought I could track them down before you had to know. But I assure you I had nothing to do with their disappearance." Every muscle in his body clenched. "No matter what Powers says."

The Colonel made damping motions with his hands. "I've accused you of nothing more than keeping the truth about my own ranch from me." He tugged on the bottom of his vest and leveled a stern gaze toward Alec. "You'll agree that you've withheld facts from me? And as to who is responsible for the theft, I merely meant it could be any of the cowboys on the Cross B. Sit down, Alec, and be reasonable. You take things too personally."

Alec resumed his seat reluctantly, the defensive anger slow to abate within him.

Trace leaned his wrists against the edge of the table. "Let's not forget Seb and his hand. Might be one of them."

Cal shook his head. "Naw, ya'll are forgetting, the only way off the Cross B is in full view of the house. How could someone drive upwards of a thousand head of cattle by here and not be noticed?"

Trace slid his empty plate back. "They couldn't."

"Then where are they hiding?" Clara stood and began gathering cutlery. "Is it possible that maybe Seb Lewis is involved somehow and trying to throw you off by pretending he's lost cattle?"

Alec considered the situation, surprised the thought hadn't occurred to him. But Seb didn't seem the type, nor did he appear to be profiting lately.

The Colonel rose. "Tomorrow I'm leaving for Boise. Alec, perhaps you boys could make a friendly call on Seb, just look around his place. We've been friends for more than ten years, and I don't think he would stoop to rustling cattle, but perhaps it would be prudent to ride down there. Seb would have the same trouble as any other rustler—how to get the cattle by here without us knowing. When I get back from my trip, we'll sit down for a full accounting and a council of war. While I'm up north, I'll make inquiries as to the movement of cattle in the area and try to see who is buying and selling."

Relief that he had someone to help shoulder the burden made Alec realize how foolish it had been to try to solve the problem on his own. He nodded. "Thank you, sir, and I do apologize for not coming to you sooner."

The Colonel clapped Alec on the shoulder on the way by. "If I didn't trust you with my ranch, Alec, I wouldn't have named you foreman."

❧

Clara worked the pump over the washtub then reached for the kettle to warm the dishwater. She needed some time alone and a chore to work off her nervous energy after that dinner.

She looked up into her own reflection in the darkened glass of the kitchen window. Her heart ached for Alec, forever struggling against what others thought of him. He took everything seriously, felt the responsibility entrusted to him as the foreman of the Cross B so heavily. His past seemed to stalk him—or was he dragging it around himself? Was part of his problem that he couldn't forget where he'd come from or how far he'd come to be the man he was today? The Colonel trusted him implicitly, and as for herself, her own feelings for him were so strong they were akin to pain.

She yelped and turned around when his face appeared over her shoulder in the window glass. Her abrupt movement almost knocked the dishes from his hands. All the air seemed sucked from the room, and her heart raced against her ribs. She took a shaky breath and tried to smile.

"I didn't mean to scare you." He held up the china cake plates. "Just thought I'd give you a hand clearing up."

The intense look in his brown eyes told Clara he was still bothered about the dinner conversation. She took the plates from him and set them on the workbench. "Thank you."

"That was good cake." He tucked his fingertips into his back pockets. "We didn't have cake the whole time you were gone, and now we've had it twice, at your homecoming party and tonight."

"But you didn't have any at my homecoming party," Clara reminded him.

He shifted his weight and looked at the floor. Whiskers shadowed his jaw, and a few dark hairs curled out of the open top of his shirt at his throat. His muscles played beneath the fabric, solid, strong. Everything about him was manly, rugged, steadfast as the canyon walls. And as remote.

Frustration welled up in her. She wanted to shock him, to break down his reserve to get to the man behind the wall. "Alec. . ." The words she'd long stifled, waiting for him to be the first to speak of their feelings, crowded out. "Alec, I know this isn't the time or the place, but I can't stand it anymore. Surely you know how I feel about you. How I've always felt about you." Her hand went out in entreaty. "Won't you say something? I love you, Alec McConnell."

He stepped back as if he'd been slapped. "Don't," his voice rasped. His retreat blocked by the table, he froze.

She moved closer. Having committed herself this far, she had to continue. "Alec, I know you feel something for me. Why won't you admit it?"

He swallowed, staring into her eyes. His chest rose and fell rapidly.

She *knew* it. He did love her. Her heart swelled. This was it. Finally he'd declare his feelings for her and take her into his arms for the kiss she'd waited for so long. She raised her face, her eyelids fluttering closed.

His hands closed on her upper arms in a viselike grip. "No. Stop it, Clara. You don't know what you're saying."

Her eyes popped open. "But I do." She leaned into him.

He groaned and closed his eyes. Then, almost as if he couldn't help himself, his arms came around her, and he crushed her to his chest. He brought his head down and claimed her lips with his own.

Clara gave herself over to the wonder of his embrace, reveling in the thud of his heart against her palms, his kiss on her lips. If only she could stay here in his arms forever. All she needed to make the moment complete was to hear the words of love from him that she longed for.

With the suddenness of being plunged into a snowbank, Alec broke the kiss and pushed Clara away from him. His breath came in gasps, and a look of shameful reproach—whether for her or for himself Clara didn't know—spread over his face.

"Alec?" she whispered.

"Clara, this isn't going to happen." His expression changed to granite. "Leave me alone. You'll regret this, and so will I. A McConnell and a Bainbridge. . .I won't do that to you or myself."

Her shock vanished in a cloud of anger at him and herself. "That's preposterous." She wanted to beat her fists against his stubborn chest and, at the same time, soothe the aching hurt blazing from his eyes. "Alec, you've got to—"

"I don't have to do anything, and I'm not going to. Just forget what happened in here."

"How can I forget? Can you? Can you forget the kiss we just shared? Can you forget that I love you?" Clara trembled with emotion.

"I can. And I will." The icy coldness in his voice froze her to the core.

She turned her back on him and gripped the edge of the dry sink. Tears cascaded down her cheeks, dropping to her hands. Humiliation trickled through her at his rejection.

She didn't turn around when the back door slammed shut.

eleven

"Trace, you head east. Cal, you take two men and make sure you sweep the high pasture. I'll cover the area between the creek and the west boundary. Those cows didn't sprout wings and fly over the canyon rim, so they're either here somewhere or they've been gotten out another way." Alec tightened the saddle cinch, jerking the strap snug.

He cast a glance toward the house, trying to ignore the cannonball sitting in his middle. The Colonel would be back tonight, and Alec had nothing of any worth to tell him. Their trip to Seb's place had snared them exactly nothing. Seb was as baffled as Alec. He'd invited Alec and his cowboys to search his property.

Cal led his mount out of the corral and leapt aboard, not bothering with the stirrup. "We've been over every inch of the ranch already. And we've been over the Double Box, too. Don't know what you expect us to find this time."

"Quit your grizzling and do as you're told." Alec regretted snapping at his youngest brother the instant the words left his mouth. He'd acted like a badger with a bunion ever since leaving Clara the week before. It was for her own good, but it sure didn't make it any easier to take. He had to be strong. She deserved better than a McConnell, and he would make sure she got it. She would get over her feelings for him if he just stayed away from her.

If only that strategy would work for him. Having her in Boston for a whole year hadn't dulled his love one bit. Seeing her every day was a pleasure that ached. Maybe he should just saddle up and ride away. Maybe go to California. But no, he owed the Colonel too much to ever leave the Cross B. He'd have to stay and deal with his feelings for Clara like a man.

"Let's go." He mounted Smoke and nudged the gray in the ribs.

Several riders fell in behind him, saddles creaking, bits jingling, and over all the steady thud of hooves on the hard, dry dirt. Riley loped at Alec's boot, tongue lolling, his stride eating up the ground.

Trace and his men veered off and plunged into the creek, sending up sheets of silvery spray. They gained the other side and galloped across the flat toward the canyon walls to the east.

When Alec's cavalcade had ridden more than a mile to the south, Cal and two riders broke off from the group and headed up the western slope to the horse meadow. Alec watched them disappear into the pines before turning to his own men. "Fan out. When you get to a draw, head up and get a count of any cattle in there. If you cut any sign or see anything suspicious, shoot into the air. You'll have to ride clear to the back of some of these draws and make sure the cattle haven't found a way up to the canyon rim and over."

The men knew better than to argue with him, but their faces clearly said they thought this a fool's errand.

Alec wheeled Smoke to head toward the nearest draw. Thick sagebrush and juniper tangled together, discouraging anyone from entering. He pulled his hat down low, put his arm up to shield his face, and headed into the undergrowth. His gelding crashed through the branches, the rich odor of sage surrounding them.

After a few yards, the foliage thinned and opened on a glade carpeted with knee-high grass. A fox skirted the tree to Alec's left, froze for an instant, then slunk off into the deep grass without so much as a whisper of sound.

Alec leaned over his mount's shoulder to survey the ground. What cow sign he found was old.

Riley nosed over the ground, zigzagging, head low, tail high. Twice he stopped before a thicket and put his nose into the breeze.

"Riley!" Alec swept his arm toward the brush.

The dog exploded into a run and dove into the bushes. Seconds later, his piercing bark filled the air, and a pair of white-faced steers plunged from the thicket into the open. Riley followed after them, herding them toward Alec.

"Two steers." Alec pursed his lips and wiped his forehead with the sleeve of his brush jacket. "We'll have to do better than that."

He and the dog followed the draw until it ended in a pile of loose shale at the base of the west canyon wall. "Not even a mountain goat could get up that grade." Alec sat his horse in the deep shadow of the wall that towered more than one hundred feet above, a looming strata of gray, red, and yellow rock. On the way back out toward Money Creek, Riley gave no sign he scented any other cattle.

Discouraged, Alec rode south. He met up with one of his cowboys coming out of a swale. "Any luck?"

"Half a dozen cows and calves. All the calves were branded, so we've already counted them once this spring." He stared at his horse's ears, not looking at Alec. "Should I keep looking? Seems like effort for nothing."

Frustration clenched Alec's middle. This foray was his last chance to find the missing cattle before a meeting with the Colonel tonight. And so far, he'd come up empty. "Keep looking." Alec's lips tightened. He didn't know which he dreaded worse, the meeting with the Colonel or facing Clara again. No, on second thought, he did know. For the thousandth time he tried to push Clara out of his mind and concentrate on the job at hand.

As the day wore on, Alec came upon pockets of Cross B cows here and there, but nothing that would raise the tally significantly. His heart lifted when he came across a group of thirty cows in a grove of trees near the creek, but the farther he rode to the south, the sparser the cattle became. By the time he reached the boundary between the Cross B and Seb Lewis's Double Box, he knew he wouldn't be able to account for even the majority of the cows they'd rounded up for branding just one month ago. He knelt beside the creek and dipped his hand into the cold water for a drink.

Riley lapped the water downstream a few yards. The shaggy dog's head came up, his wet nose twitching. He cocked his ears toward the northeast.

Alec rose and strained his eyes. Nothing moved on the flat ground across the creek. Not a breath of air stirred the grasses. Clouds a mile high piled up in the sky, fluffy and white, hanging on nothing. Smoke stamped his hoof and shook his neck until the bit rattled.

A faint pop sounded in the distance across the creek. Then another. Rifle shots? He'd best go check it out.

Unease settled in Alec's chest. The shots had been pretty faint. He tested the wind, his thoughts tumbling. Which direction had the shots come from—the east side of the creek or the west? Cal had two riders with him on the west slope. Trace was alone on the east. Best check on Trace first. Though Trace was a crack shot with that rifle of his and more than capable of taking care of himself, if he had stumbled upon something, Alec hoped the middle McConnell brother had sense enough to wait for the rest of the crew before taking it on.

Alec mounted and urged Smoke into the creek. The

gelding went willingly into the water and scrambled up the east bank. Riley bounded ahead of the horse, loping across the flat in the direction of the shots.

A mile or so up the creek, Alec met up with Cal and two Cross B cowboys plowing through the creek below the horse pasture. Cal's voice carried across the open space. "I heard shots."

"Must be Trace."

Cal must've felt the same unease as Alec, for he leaned over his horse's neck and kicked him into a lope. Smoke jumped beneath Alec in pursuit. Together they headed north along the creek, the other riders falling in behind.

A few cows dotted this open plain and scattered in their wake. Alec made a mental note of them. At this time of the year, this wide, grassy bowl should be overrun with Cross B cattle.

Relief coursed through Alec when Trace's horse appeared from the scrub under the canyon's eastern wall. Still more than a half mile distant, Trace sat slack in the saddle. Trace's mount stopped and began cropping grass.

Cal eased back on the reins. "Guess he's going to wait for us to come to him."

Alec slowed Smoke and pulled him alongside Cal's mount. "Yep, doesn't look like he's in a hurry. Can't be too urgent."

Trace kept his head down, as if studying his hands.

Alec's brows came down. Was he holding something he'd found or just looking at his rifle across the saddle in front of himself? The rock formation marking the entrance to Skull Canyon loomed over Trace's shoulder a quarter mile or more to the north.

"Hey, you napping?" Cal called out as soon as they got close. "Wake up. We heard your shots. Sorry it took us so long to get here, but I was almost to the west wall."

Trace wobbled in the saddle and alarm spiraled up Alec's spine. Deathly pale, Trace blinked once, slowly, and his lips moved. His rifle clattered from his hands onto the rocky ground.

"What is it, Trace?"

In response, Trace slid from the saddle into a heap on the ground.

Alec vaulted off Smoke and ran to his brother's side. Gently, he rolled Trace onto his back. Trace's coat fell open. Fiery ice shot through Alec's veins. A large, red blotch decorated the lower left half of Trace's shirt.

❧

Clara shut the calf-pen gate and brushed bits of straw from her skirt. Raising her hand, she shielded her eyes against the glare of the sun and scanned the valley floor for signs of riders. Heat shimmered in the air above the grass, making distant objects waver and disappear. She tugged a handkerchief from her sleeve and mopped her face and neck. At least she was finally using a handkerchief for something other than to dry her tears. She must've cried buckets since Alec broke her heart. The cad.

"Hello."

She jumped. "Oh, Steadman. Hello. I wasn't expecting you. Are you here to see the Colonel? He's not due back until tonight."

"Pardon the intrusion. I stopped by the house, but no one was home." He swept his hat from his head and bowed. "I've come to see you, actually. That is, if you'll permit such boldness. I've just taken delivery of a buggy, and all it needs is a lady as lovely as yourself to grace it on an inaugural outing. Do say you'll come."

The buggy gleamed with shiny newness, black paint so glossy it looked wet, yellow wheels decorated with tiny red scrolls of color. Even the harness looked new with bright metal stampings throwing back the sunshine like sparks. The bay trotter shook its head.

What a perfect opportunity to show Alec McConnell she didn't care. "I'd love a buggy ride. Can you wait a few moments while I change into something more appropriate?" She hurried to the house and lost no time slipping into one of her Boston day dresses. Her hair, already escaping the twist she'd fashioned that morning, tumbled down around her shoulders when she pulled the dress over her head. She took time to brush it out and pin it up, knowing Steadman would anticipate a bit of a wait for a "proper young lady."

When she returned, he appraised her with an approving gleam in his eye and assisted her into the buggy. He spread a linen dust robe over her lap, and with a flick of the whip, they were off.

Clara tried to ignore the ache in her chest over Alec and enjoy the ride. Alec had made himself quite clear. The stubborn oaf. Resolved to be a pleasant companion for Steadman, she gave him a bright smile.

"You look very fetching in that costume, Clara. Like a rose among the thorns, living with all those men on the ranch without any female company to comfort you. Do you miss Boston?"

Did she miss Boston? Narrow curvy streets, buildings, people, bustle everywhere she turned. And rules. Rules for eating, rules for proper attire, rules for who could speak to whom in society. Binding Clara's outgoing spirit until she hardly recognized herself.

"No, I can't say that I do. I'm grateful to my father for wanting me to see more of the world than Idaho Territory, but I don't miss the city." She lifted her eyes to the wide expanse of blue overhead and breathed deep the pine and sage in the air. "This is the most beautiful place on earth. This is home."

The horse trotted swiftly, neck arched, legs flashing. Steadman spoke of his home in St. Paul and of his desire to build his ranch into an enviable property. "I want people to look at me and say, 'That's Steadman Devers. His ranch is the best in the territory.'"

"Lofty ambitions. I'm sure you'll make it. You have a good start already." Clara ignored the niggle of unease in the back of her mind. It wasn't wrong to be ambitious. A man needed ambition to make something of himself in the West.

Devers flipped the reins against the trotter's rump. "Tell me about the Cross B. How long have you lived there?"

"Since I was a child. My earliest memories are of living in the little two-roomed cabin just in back of where the bunkhouse sits now. We had a sod barn and only a couple of ranch hands. It seemed my father spent all day out on the range. Sometimes my mother teased him that he loved his cows more than he loved us. But he spends more time traveling now than he does at the ranch. He's interested in politics and is good friends with Governor Irwin. He leaves most of the running of the ranch to Alec." His name faltered on her lips.

"I understand your mother passed away a year ago?"

Familiar sorrow trickled through Clara. "Yes, a riding accident. She was trying to find a way through Skull Canyon. It was an obsession with her—finding a pathway between your ranch and ours."

"Why would that have mattered? Why search for something like that? She could've taken the long way around like we're doing."

Clara fingered the edge of the lap robe, pleating and releasing it while she considered what to say. "I think she was bored. And if I admit it, a little spoiled perhaps. She loved to ride, she loved a challenge, and she set her mind to finding a passage. My father blames himself for her death. He gave her the horse, and he laughed at her notion that there was a way through. I don't think he's gotten over it. He even fenced off the mouth of the canyon after she died. No one's been in there since, though I intend to try myself soon."

"Perhaps you should leave things as they are. Sparks tells me that whole area is unstable. Rock slides, loose stones, narrow, winding gullies—it isn't safe in there. You'd best listen to your father. I wouldn't want you to get hurt." Steadman turned the horse under the crossbeam gate to his ranch. "Do you like the new sign? Sparks made it."

A slab of wood branded with the Lazy P mark hung from the crossbeam, swinging gently in the breeze. "Very nice."

"Thank you. I'll tell Sparks you approve. Now, in the hope that you would come on the drive, I instructed my cook to lay out some refreshments." He stopped the buggy in front of the large house and hopped down.

The eager look in his eyes unsettled Clara. She glanced at the wide porch and tall windows. "Will anyone be joining us?" She placed her hand in his and stepped out of the buggy.

"Not today, though if it would make you feel better, we could sit on the porch instead of going into the house." He tucked her arm into the crook of his elbow and led her up the stairs.

She thrust aside her misgivings. Steadman had proven to be a perfect gentleman. "Of course not. You have a beautiful parlor. I'd love to see it again."

The richly appointed room welcomed her, and she took the same seat as she had on her previous visit. A tea table stood to the side, laden with food. "Steadman, I felt I should apologize for the other night. Thank you for being so tactful, and I'm sorry I didn't get to show you out. It's these missing cattle. Alec hasn't been able to find out where they're disappearing to, and I'm afraid it's made him rather defensive."

Steadman was off his chair in a trice, kneeling before her. "Clara, let's not talk about cattle or Alec. I have something else on my mind."

He took her hands, and the move surprised her so much she allowed it.

"Clara, I've known since the moment I saw you on the stage that you were a woman of quality, a woman I could easily fall in love with. And I have. I know this is sudden, and I do intend to speak to your father, but I can't hold back any longer. Clara Bainbridge, will you marry me?" He lifted her hands and kissed her knuckles.

She blinked and slowly withdrew her fingers from his grasp. Her mouth opened, but no words came out.

"I can see I've taken your breath away, dear Clara." He pressed his palms into the upholstery on either side of her, blocking her escape. "But I promise you, I'm serious." He leaned closer, his face only inches from hers.

Only last night she had seen Alec's beloved face from this distance, had felt the crush of being held in his arms, his lips tight against hers. At the last instant before Steadman could kiss her, she turned her head and leaned away. "Steadman, no."

"Please?" His hand came up to clasp her chin and turn it back toward him. "One kiss. Surely you won't begrudge me one little kiss, after I've gone to all this trouble? You can't say my intentions aren't honorable. I did ask you to marry me first." His fingers tightened, and he bent his head once more.

Her hands came up to push against his chest, but before she could, the front door crashed open.

Steadman sprang back. He relaxed when his foreman

stalked through the doorway.

Clara stood up and hurried around the settee, placing it between her and Steadman. Gratitude toward Sparks for interrupting them flowed over her, making her weak. She didn't fault Steadman, and his proposal, though it had caught her off guard, had gratified that wounded part of her heart still suffering from Alec's rejection. Perhaps she should've allowed the kiss. And yet, the thought made her stomach lurch.

"Boss, you got a minute?" Dust sifted from his sweat-dampened clothes, and dirt streaked his face. His eyes darted to Clara, and he swept his hat from his head. "Ma'am." He looked back to Steadman and inclined his head toward the front porch.

Steadman bowed slightly to Clara. "If you will excuse me for a moment, Clara, I will speak to my foreman. Then we can resume our conversation." He followed Sparks out and closed the pocket doors behind him.

Clara's shoulders wilted in relief. She tried to gather her scattered attention. A proposal. What would her father say? What would Alec say? A bitter laugh caught in her throat. It didn't matter a whit what Alec said. Her chin came up. He'd made that perfectly clear. Clara circled the settee and resumed her seat. She spread her skirts just so and folded her hands in her lap to await Steadman's return.

After what seemed a long time, he came back to the parlor. He smiled at her and took her hand between his. His eyes stared intently into hers. "Clara, I fear I won't be able to see you home. Something's come up. I'll have one of my men return you to the Cross B right away." He advanced to stand before her.

She swallowed, her mouth dry.

"And I apologize profusely for my forward behavior. I was

overcome by being so near you. Please say you will consider my proposal. I'll be over to speak to your father at the first opportunity."

He stepped aside and motioned for her to precede him into the hall.

Sparks had left the foyer, and at the foot of the porch stairs, a hunched, grizzled old man stood beside the buggy.

"Toolie will see you home safely. I apologize again that I can't take you myself." Steadman handed her up into the seat.

Clara breathed a sigh of relief when they passed under the Lazy P sign and trotted up the main road. Her thoughts turned faster than the buggy wheels all the way back to the ranch.

She arrived at the same time as the doctor. . .

twelve

Alec stood in the corner of the room, arms folded, concentrating on the doctor. Dr. Hanrahan had a brogue thick enough to saw into planks. Alec missed Doc Jeffers, the Civil War veteran army surgeon who used to be the town physician. He didn't know this new fellow. Was he any good?

Cal leaned his shoulder against the wall beside Alec, dark blotches of their brother's blood smeared across his faded, blue shirt. "Think he'll make it?" Cal whispered.

"Trace is tough. He'll make it." Alec shifted, his gaze moving to the side of the bed where Clara sat holding Trace's limp hand between hers.

Worry formed lines on her brow, and she gnawed her lower lip. When she'd heard Trace was injured, she'd flown up the stairs and refused to be dislodged from his bedside, propriety or not.

Trace lay in the middle of the bed—the Colonel's bed—where Clara had said to bring him when they finally reached the ranch.

Alec remembered every step of the long journey to the main house, Trace jouncing along on the makeshift travois they'd cobbled together. Alec had sent one of the men ahead to fetch the sheriff and the doctor. The doctor had come right away. The ranch hand arrived later saying Sheriff Powers had said he couldn't come right now. He had a line on the stage robbers and was headed to Silver City. He wouldn't be back until the next day. Alec burned at this news—further proof that McConnells weren't high on Powers's list unless they needed to be arrested for something.

The Colonel arrived almost on the heels of the doctor and stood in the doorway, his face haggard. The scene brought back so many memories to Alec, he could only imagine what the Colonel was seeing in his mind. Old Doc Jeffers bent over this same bed tending another injured person. Only that time, no physician could save her. Mrs. Bainbridge hadn't even awakened to tell her family good-bye. Alec would never forget the ranch-wide search when Mrs. Bainbridge hadn't come back from a ride. Her battered body at the base of a pile of rocky rubble, the smell of dirt and dust hanging in the air, even hours later, from the landslide that had caught her and her horse.

Alec swallowed and shifted again. Anger bubbled under the stoic expression he tried to maintain. "As soon as we know he's going to live, I'm heading out to track down the scum who shot him."

Cal nodded, rolling his hat brim between his hands, staring down at it. "Night's coming on. Maybe we should wait until he wakes up. He might be able to tell us something about who did this."

Alec knew Cal spoke wisely, but everything in him chafed at the wait. Every minute they lingered here gave the enemy more time to escape and hide his tracks. Alec pushed aside the curtain to check the angle of the descending sun. "It might be a while before he wakes up."

"I still think it's best to wait." Cal jammed his hat onto his head, then seemed to remember he was in the house and yanked it off again. "I don't plan to stray too far until I know if he's going to be all right."

Alec gave Cal a hard look. How could he even think that Trace wouldn't pull through this? "*When* he wakes up, we'll have to tie him to the bed to keep him from going after whoever did this."

The doctor finally stepped away from the bed and dunked his hands into the basin on the washstand.

Alec peered at Trace. His brother's chest moved with his breathing. He was still alive. Alec swallowed hard. "Well?" His voice came out harsher than he'd intended.

"The bullet went straight through his side. Nicked the spleen, but I think I've stopped the bleeding." Dr. Hanrahan wiped his hands on the roller towel. "He's a brawny lad, strong as a plow horse. It's too soon to tell, but if I was a betting man, I'd put a small wager down that he'll pull through. Infection is the enemy now. You'll have to watch him close. I expect he'll battle a fever before this is decided one way or another. If he can get through the first few days, he'll make it."

Clara's eyes glistened, and she wiped tears from her cheeks. "When will he wake up, Doctor?"

He shook his head. "Best he should sleep for now. He'll be hurting something terrible once he comes to himself. You'll want to watch for fever, miss. Bathe him with cool cloths and give him a wee bit of this laudanum." He held up a bottle from his bag. "But only a wee bit, mind you. The blood loss will give him a mighty thirst. Water at first, then a little broth as he begins to heal."

Alec stepped over and held out his hand. "Thanks, Doc."

Hanrahan turned to Clara. "I understand you've recently been to Boston. I pray you won't think me too forward in asking, but as I took my training at Harvard, I was hoping I might call on you in the future and we could talk about Boston."

Jealousy pricked Alec then jabbed him when Clara's face lit with a smile. "Of course. That would be nice."

Cal and the Colonel saw the doctor out of the house.

Alec picked up a chair and brought it to Trace's bedside. He straddled the chair and crossed his arms along the back.

Clara cast him a quick glance, then dipped a cloth in a bowl of water and wrung it out. She began washing some of the dirt from Trace's face and neck. "You don't have to sit with him." She cleaned a cut on the back of Trace's hand. "I'll stay and watch."

Was she trying to get rid of him? "I'd rather stay."

That night was one of the longest of Alec's life. He sat beside his brother, concentrating on the rise and fall of Trace's chest, hoping and praying his brother would recover, would open his eyes and tell Alec who had done this and why.

Deep in the night, Trace's fever soared, his skin paper-dry and flushed. Clara bathed his face and neck again and again with cool cloths.

Cal kept vigil in the hall, his boots thudding dully on the carpet runner. He also kept Clara supplied with fresh water. Each time he entered with a full pitcher, he sent a questioning look to Alec, who shook his head.

The inactivity forced on him by logic ate at Alec. He should be out tracking down whoever shot Trace, not sitting here doing nothing. And where was Powers? Alec knew good and well that if anyone else besides a McConnell had been shot, Powers would've been burning up the trail to get there. The animosity between Alec and Powers might lead to Trace's attacker getting away.

Alec's anger flared. Being a McConnell had never been more costly.

❧

Clara's hands ached from wringing out the cloths. The tips of her fingers puckered from their long exposure to the water. But she couldn't stop. Knowing Trace would hate this invasion of his privacy, but needing to do all she could to reduce his fever, she folded the sheet down to his waist and sponged his chest and arms. She kept her eyes down, not looking at Alec. Fear for Trace, frustration at Alec, and confusion over Steadman's startling proposal all collided and tangled with the growing weariness that tugged at her limbs and weighed down her eyelids.

"I'll do that for a while." Alec took the cloth from her hand. "Why don't you go to bed? You look beat."

She smoothed her hair away from her face and took out one of her combs and reinserted it tighter. What did it matter how she looked or how tired she was? In spite of herself, she tried to perk up, straightening her shoulders and blinking hard. "I'll stay. But we can take turns cooling him." If he thought she looked tired, he should take a gander at himself. Deep lines etched his face, and shadows hung under his eyes.

The rift between them seemed wider than Money Creek Canyon. Nothing between them would ever be the same. Clara chided herself. She shouldn't be worried about that now. She should be thinking about Trace. And yet, she couldn't help herself. Alec dominated her thoughts as always.

Lamplight cast shadows across his face as he tended Trace. She knew every plane and angle, every expression. How long had she loved him? Since the first time she saw him, rigid with indignation at being behind bars, defiant and trying to be brave in front of his brothers. Unlike Trace and Cal, who had leapt at the chance to come to the Cross B, Alec had resisted, not wanting to be beholden to anyone. He refused to let Clara—or anyone else—get close for a long time. It wasn't until he gave his heart to God that he allowed anyone inside the walls he'd set up around his heart.

"Don't worry, Clara," her mama had said when Alec walked away from Clara's first attempts at friendship. "He just needs some time. He's carrying around a powerful hurt right now. He'll come around."

He had. Or so she thought. After a year at the ranch, a

long year of being patient, Alec had changed. Immersing himself in ranch life, drinking in knowledge from the seasoned hands, he became a first-rate cowboy. When the Colonel made him the ramrod of the Cross B, Clara didn't know who was more proud, Alec or her father.

Alec had gradually changed toward Clara, too. He looked out for her, finding little ways to show he cared. Saddling her horse for her, bringing her interesting rocks, showing her a bird's nest hidden in the tall grass, or helping her care for the orphaned calves. And cinnamon candy sticks. On his rare trips to town, he never forgot. Not even once. And he'd given her his most prized possession—his pocketknife. How could she help but fall in love with him?

And yet, though she *knew*—especially after his kiss last night—that he cared for her, he held himself back. Clara closed her eyes and laid her head against the chair back. As stubborn as Alec was, she knew she'd never break through the stockade around his heart. If she was to get inside, he would have to open the door and invite her in.

Sleep tugged at her, jumbling her thoughts.

❧

Alec replaced the damp cloth on Trace's forehead for the hundredth time. His brother relaxed a bit, and his breathing became deeper, more restful. Alec's stomach muscles loosened. He glanced up at Clara.

A flush of sleep lay on her cheeks, and her hair was slowly coming out of its twist. Her dark lashes stood out against her skin, and her lips moved slightly as if she were speaking in her dreams.

Immediately, he was back in the kitchen, holding her in his arms, savoring her kiss and trying to rein in his galloping heart. That same heart now throbbed as if pierced by a Ute arrow. Breaking that kiss, breaking her heart, had been the hardest thing he'd ever done. But he was what he was, and he'd never link his name with hers, his past with hers.

A big part of his past lurched into the room like an apparition. Alec blinked, wondering if he was dreaming. He shot to his feet, knocking his chair to the floor.

Angus McConnell hung on the doorjamb, shaking. Unshaven, filthy, eyes so bloodshot it hurt to look at them. When he staggered into the room, he reeked of spirits and filth from ten feet away.

"What are you doing here?" Alec braced his feet apart and stood between his father and his brother's bed. "Get out."

"I come to see my boy." Angus raised a bony finger and pointed it at Alec's nose. "I heard in town he'd been shot. I come to see how he is. Took me all night to get here."

Alec stooped and righted his chair. The anger caused by the hard-packed path his thoughts had tread all night boiled up. "You've got a nerve coming here. Trying to salve your conscience? It's too late for that. Don't pretend you care, not after a lifetime of ignoring us."

Angus tried to move around Alec, but Alec wouldn't allow him. "Trace doesn't want to see you any more than I do. Just get out of here. Crawl back into whatever bottle you were soaking in and leave us alone."

"Alec, please." Clara rounded the foot of the bed. "Trace is his son."

Alec gritted his teeth and spoke through stiff lips. "Stay out of this." He grabbed Angus by the collar and marched him to the door. "Get out, old man. Don't come back here again." They collided with Cal in the doorway.

Cal backed up a pace, nose wrinkling when he caught a whiff of Angus. "Hello, Pa." Cal's words were laced with sarcasm.

Angus flailed at the end of Alec's grip, but he was no

match for his much larger, much stronger, sober son. His hands connected with nothing.

"Get him out of here." Alec thrust Angus toward Cal. Cal took his father by the arm and pulled him toward the stairs. Howling and swearing, Angus protested all the way out into the gray dawn.

Alec whirled on his boot heel to look at the bed. His chest heaved, and his fists clenched taut, making his arms shake.

"Alec, was that necessary? All he wanted was to see his son." She bent over Trace, laying her palm against his chest. She straightened and her glare shot through Alec like blue darts.

"He doesn't deserve to see him."

Clara stepped close to Alec and gripped his arm, giving it a shake. "What is the matter with you?"

"Don't touch me. Stay away from me, Clara. Can't you see McConnells are damaged goods? What other proof do you need?"

She stepped back as if he'd struck her, and he couldn't have felt worse if he had. She lifted her chin, and her lower lip trembled for an instant. "You're right. You are damaged goods."

thirteen

Her words slammed into Alec's gut. It was one thing to say it himself, but another to hear it from the lips of the woman he loved more than life itself.

"You *are* damaged goods. But not for the reason you think." Emotion thickened her voice. "Yes, your father is a drunk. Yes, once you were a thief, and you've spent time in jail. And yes, some people only want to remember that you're one of those bad McConnell boys. But that's not what is damaging you. It's your unforgiving spirit. You can't forgive the town. You can't forgive your father, and most of all, you can't forgive yourself. You throw all your energy into despising your father and yourself. Your hatred of Angus McConnell is eating away at your soul. You can't see anything else when you look at him. You have no pity, no charity, just hatred. It taints everything in your life."

"Pity? Charity?" He nearly choked on the words. "After what he did to us? What he still does to us with his drinking? Do you think Money Creek will ever see us as anything different when he's a constant and colorful reminder of what bad seed we come from?"

Her hands tightened on the end rail of the bed. "Alec, you think your father and your past bind you with chains and fetters you can't break. But that's not true. Nothing binds you but yourself. Can't you see? You have to start with forgiveness. If you don't forgive your father and yourself, you'll be a cripple for the rest of your life. You have to lay that burden down."

Just like that. Lay the burden down. His life wasn't some church hymn, all tidy by the chorus and hallelujah. It wasn't as simple as that. "You're naive. Just like your mother. She said the same thing to me once. She didn't know what she was talking about, and neither do you. You should keep out of things that don't concern you."

Clara straightened to her full height and looked him square in the eye, tears pooling on her lashes. "You wouldn't know the truth if you ran over it in the street. I guess I made a lucky escape. Steadman Devers might not be the man of my dreams, but at least when I marry him, I won't be tying myself to a great, unfeeling hulk like you."

"Marry him?" All the air seemed to suck out of the room. Alec reeled back like he'd been gut-punched.

"That's right. He proposed to me. I thought I couldn't marry him, not when I—" She faltered, her cheeks flushing with pink. "Not when I thought I loved you. But now I see you for what you are. I couldn't love a man so unforgiving, so hard-hearted. What if I ever did something to displease you? Would you turn on me the same way? You've managed to kill any love I felt for you." She swept past him and left him staring after her.

Alec bowed his head. Tension drained from his muscles, leaving him sore and limp, empty and alone. Clara was going to marry Steadman Devers? A cold wind blew through his frame.

Trace grunted, the first sound he'd made since being carried into the house. "I know who shot me. . .and why." Trace's words sounded forced. His jaw muscles stood out, his teeth clamped tight.

Every nerve in Alec's body came alive. "Trace." Relief that his brother was awake and talking surged along his veins. Then the words registered. "Who?"

"That foreman of Devers's. Sparks. I came across him near the gate to Skull Canyon, and I followed him. I think he's been driving cows into Skull."

Alec blinked. What was Sparks doing on this side of the Stovepipes? A tiny flame of hope at having a direction to look, a clue to follow, lit in Alec's middle. He narrowed his eyes. Driving cattle into Skull Canyon. His mind raced. Driving into or driving through? Had Sparks found a way through? Alec hadn't set foot in the canyon in over a year, since he helped the Colonel put up the fence. It hadn't occurred to him to even scout around in Skull, because he knew it was impassable. And what he had assumed to be true almost cost Trace his life. He fisted his hands. Time to make a call on the Lazy P, and this time, he wouldn't be going around the long way.

Trace pierced Alec with his gray eyes. "Whatever you're planning, I'm going with you. I have a score to settle with that Sparks fellow." He put his palms against the mattress and tried to raise himself. A groan tore from his lips. "My insides feel like they're on fire."

Alec put his hand on Trace's shoulder and gently forced him down on the bed. "You're not going anywhere. I'll rope you to this bed if I have to. The doc said you're to stay put." He reached for the bottle of laudanum on the bedside and pulled out the stopper. "Here, the doc left you this for the pain." He helped Trace lift his head and take a swallow.

Trace grimaced. "Stuff tastes like horse liniment." A sheen of sweat coated his pallid face. "Alec?"

"Yeah?"

"Clara's right about you, you know."

Alec looked up from replacing the medicine bottle on the table. His brother's lips pressed in a line that bespoke the pain he was in. Alec stepped to his side. "Trace, you need to rest. You shouldn't be worrying about anything now but getting well."

"Don't change the subject. Clara's right." Trace's lids lifted, exposing his steely-gray eyes. "You gotta let it go, Alec. Your spitting at Pa isn't hurting him near as much as it's hurting you."

Anger flared anew in Alec's chest. Each mention of their father was like touching a wound. "Don't tell me how to deal with Pa."

Trace pressed his hand to his side and took shallow breaths. "I forgot. Nobody can tell you anything. Just like Pa. McConnells are stubborn, but you take the prize. You aren't really mad at Pa. You're mad at yourself. You just take your mad out on him. Him and the townsfolk. And now Clara."

"I do not. And I'm not anything like Pa." Alec spat out the words. The very idea left a foul taste in his mouth. That Trace would compare him to a drunken, abusive lout of a man turned his stomach.

"Pa's a bitter, unforgiving man who won't listen to the truth when it's shouting in his face. He's never forgiven Ma for dying on him. He's never forgiven himself for needing to drink himself sick to forget. And he's never forgiven himself for not raising us better. He blames himself for us going wild and landing in jail." Trace coughed, his face contorting with pain.

Alec poured him a glass of water and held it to his lips.

"Thanks. Take a long, hard look at yourself, Alec, before it's too late. If you don't change, you're going to wind up just like him. Shriveled up and miserable." He lay back, bathed in sweat, face screwed up in pain.

"I've never heard you talk this much. You finished digging your spurs into me?" He tugged the sheet up to Trace's chest.

"Just about." Trace closed his eyes again, seeming to sink into the bed a little at Alec's stubbornness. "Don't let Clara slip through your hands. I know you think you're not good enough for her, that a McConnell can never be good enough for her, but you will be, if you let God help you forgive Pa. And if you accept that God has forgiven you and you forgive yourself, you're the match of any man in the territory. You owe it to yourself, and you owe it to Clara, who loves you in spite of you being a stubborn mule. Save her from making a mistake. That Eastern dandy is not the man for our Clara."

Alec said nothing.

He turned to go, but once more Trace stopped him, this time with a whisper. "Alec, be careful, won't you?"

"I will, little brother."

❧

Clara dug her heels into Hawkwing's sides and leaned far over his neck. His black mane lashed her face, swiping her tears. Chilly dawn wind rushed over her. Together they raced north along the creek toward town, but no matter how fast they went, she couldn't escape the pain in her heart. Alec's rejection of her was complete.

Listening in the hallway outside the sickroom probably wasn't ethical, but she was glad she had. Steadman had to be told about Sparks. Together they could go to the sheriff.

A little thrill of vindication surged through her. After all this time, her mother's conviction that a way existed through Skull Canyon had been proven true. A band of grief fell from Clara's chest, one she hadn't even known existed. It had always saddened her that her mother's quest had never been finished.

She followed the rutted town road until she reached the crossing. Money Creek tumbled and purled in the morning sun, throwing back sparkles of early morning sunlight to reflect on the undersides of the willows and aspens lining the banks. Hawkwing rushed into the ford without hesitation.

Cold creek water rose up, splashing her skirts and her mount's flanks. She urged him on, clinging to him as he scrambled up the far bank. Clara took a moment to revel in the freedom of racing on a fast horse across the valley floor. She'd only ridden a few times since she'd come home. Now she left the road behind and headed across country, rounding the lower shoulders of the Stovepipe Hills and turning southeast into the valley that held Steadman Devers's ranch. Her horse eased back from a gallop to a trot.

She had to tell Steadman about the traitor in his midst. . . and tell him of her intention not to accept his proposal of marriage. Though she'd spouted off to Alec in her hurt and frustration that she meant to marry Steadman, she knew it wouldn't be right.

She moistened her lips and tucked a stray strand of hair behind her ear. Hawkwing dropped to a walk, as if sensing her mood. A large part of her heart, the part that had belonged to Alec, lay frozen as a winter pond inside her. She didn't love Steadman. He generated none of the breathless, tingling excitement she felt whenever she encountered Alec McConnell. No, if she couldn't have Alec, she'd settle for no one.

❧

Alec led Smoke from the corral. Cal followed with Coyote, a dun cow pony with an ugly disposition, but who could go all day without stopping. The flinty look in his younger brother's eyes reassured Alec. Cross B hands saddled up around them.

"Deuce, you beat it into town and see if Powers has come back from Silver City yet. Have him come around through Skull Canyon from the east side. If what I think is true, me and Cal and the boys can head in from the west and hopefully trap a rustling crew between us. If they aren't there, we'll head toward Devers's place. Sparks most likely won't be expecting us to have figured it out. He's probably banking on his shot having killed Trace before he could tell us anything. The Colonel will stay here to guard Trace, just in case someone tries to finish the job."

"Sure, boss. It'll take us some time."

"We'll sit tight on our end for as long as we can."

"Don't round up all those rustlers before I get there." Deuce swung into the saddle, his face grim.

"We'll save the biggest, baddest one for you." Cal dropped his stirrup into place.

"Give me a horse."

Alec turned. His father clung to a fencepost for support. Familiar disgust clawed up Alec's rib cage. Forgiveness was the last thing on his mind. He wanted to tell Angus that walking back to town would be just the thing to sober him up, but he held back. He didn't have time for an argument.

"Take one from the corral. Leave it at the livery stable." Alec rechecked his cinch then slid his rifle into the scabbard. He checked his gun belt. Plenty of extra ammunition.

"I ain't going to town. I want a horse, and I want a rifle." Angus squinted at him through one half-closed eye. "I'm going with you to get the man who shot my son."

Cal snorted. "You wouldn't last ten minutes in the saddle. Go back to town."

"I'm not drunk. One way or another, I'm going with you." He looked as if one gust of wind would topple him.

"I don't have time to nursemaid you." Alec handed Cal his reins. "We'll be riding hard. If you drop back, you're on your own. Saddle a horse. I'll get you a gun." He didn't know why he even entertained the thought of bringing Angus along. He only knew he didn't have time to argue about it. He had to get to Sparks before the man skipped the territory. His boots echoed on the barn floor as he headed toward the gun rack in the tack room.

On his way back to Cal, gripping a Winchester in one hand and a box of shells in the other, he paused before the last stall. The half door stood wide open. Hawkwing should be dozing in there.

"Hey, Alec?" Cal stalked around the corner and stopped, looking into the stall. "Looks like Clara took Hawkwing out this morning."

Alec pushed aside all Trace's words about Clara and stepped out into the sunshine, Cal on his heels. He didn't have time to brood over all that now. "She probably just went for a ride to cool down. She was pretty mad when she left."

Cal grabbed a handful of Coyote's mane, leaping astride and fitting his boots into the stirrups. "I heard her holler at you, but I was too busy hustling Pa out of the house to get the gist of the rumpus. Looks like she headed toward town."

He cocked an eyebrow at Alec, who ignored him and swung aboard Smoke. "Quit jawing, and let's ride." He whistled for Riley and kicked Smoke into a lope, heading across the valley floor to Skull Canyon. He'd deal with the rustlers first then figure out how to deal with Clara.

fourteen

In spite of his vow not to nursemaid his father on this ride, Alec found himself twisting in the saddle from time to time to see if the old man still followed. Each time he checked, Angus's horse had drifted a little farther back, but he remained in sight.

Riley ran alongside Alec's stirrup, tongue lolling, eyes bright. Nobody spoke on the ride to Skull Canyon.

Alec pulled up beside the gate to let the horses catch their breath.

Cal took down his canteen and pressed it to his lips. "Gonna be another scorcher. Sure wish this weather would break."

Alec wiped his face with his forearm. Already the air shimmered in the middle-distance, baking the ground under the eye-squinting sun. He slipped from his horse and checked his cinch again. They would be heading through rough territory. He couldn't risk his saddle sliding.

Around him, his men did the same.

He cast a glance toward his pa, leaning over his mount's neck, eyes closed, braced on his stacked hands on the saddle horn. A liverish cast to his features and a quiver to his thin lips bespoke his ill health. Stubborn old man. Why had he bothered to come? He was nothing but a liability. Alec shrugged and turned away. He poured some water into his hand and let Riley lap it up.

Trace's words and Clara's accusations about being un-forgiving bored through Alec's mind. Without stopping to examine his feelings, he took the canteen over to Angus. "Here, take a drink."

Surprise coated Angus's features. He clasped the canteen with a shaky hand, lifted it to his lips, and took a brief swallow. "Thanks, son." His words came out a croaking whisper. "Been a while since I had water."

Alec bit back the sarcastic words that leapt to his tongue. Instead, he stoppered the canteen and stalked back to his horse. "Let's go, boys."

They rode into Skull Canyon. Alec kept an eye on both the trail and the rim above. If he was setting up an ambush, this would be the perfect place.

Sparks. Alec pieced together what he knew of the man. According to Devers, Sparks had been running the Lazy P for the last year and a half. Had he been stealing cattle all that time? But how had he stumbled upon a way through Skull Canyon? Were there Double Box and Cross B cattle grazing with the Lazy P herd, or was Sparks holding them somewhere else? Devers was such a greenhorn, he'd probably never notice stolen cattle in his herd. Alec's gut twisted at the thought of Clara marrying Steadman Devers.

The going narrowed as they wound farther into the maze of gullies and gashes in the rock. Sparks had taken the time to try to eliminate some of the cow sign near to the gate, but once they were out of sight of the fence, it became evident that this path was well used. Driving cattle single file through this cut must've taken ages.

Rounding a tight bend, the trail widened and opened up a bit. The rockslide that had taken Mrs. Bainbridge's life came into view. He hadn't seen it in more than a year, and time and human effort had changed the landscape. Slabs of rock had been pushed aside and a clear trail carved through the debris. Trees and brush felled in the initial landslip lay twisted in the rubble, roots pointed skyward, leaves brittle and brown. Someone had gone to a lot of trouble to make the trail suitable for moving cattle. Farther along, fresher cascades of rock and rubble piled like tailings from a hard-rock mine.

Cal pointed to the rocky walls. "Look, rock drill marks. Somebody dynamited here."

Alec studied the vertical grooves. "With all the blasting we've heard since the new mineral strikes were found around Money Creek, it's no wonder we didn't notice a couple blasts way back in here."

Riley cocked his ears and lifted his nose, snuffling the air. A quiver ran through his body.

Alec pulled up, raising his hand to stop those following. He snapped his fingers to bring Riley close before the dog could bark or run into the cut.

The dog danced near, eager for Alec's command.

Alec slipped from the saddle and motioned for his riders to do the same. The faint smell of wood smoke drifted toward them. And when Alec held his breath, he thought he caught the sound of cattle.

"From here on out we go on foot. Look sharp. I'll go first with the dog."

ॐ

Clara tethered her horse to the post beside the front steps to Steadman's home. She took a moment to dust her riding skirt and smooth her hair before lifting the brass door knocker and giving it three sharp raps.

She stepped back in surprise when Sparks answered. His eyes bored into hers, and he held the door open only the width of his body. "Howdy, Miss Bainbridge. What can I do for you?"

Her throat constricted, and she had to force herself not to turn tail and run. It took all her control to look this rustler in the eye. His sharp stare made her skin prickle. "Mr. Sparks. I came to see Steadman. Is he in?"

"He's real busy right now. Can you come back later?" He inched the door closed a bit farther.

"I'm afraid I must insist. I've ridden all this way with an urgent message." She flashed him her most engaging smile, praying she didn't look as nervous as she felt.

"Who is it, Sparks?"

Relief at hearing Steadman's voice made Clara's knees wobble. He wouldn't let anything happen to her. If she could just get him alone to explain about Sparks. "Steadman?" She raised her voice, standing on tiptoe to see around the foreman. He blocked her way again.

"Why, Clara, what a pleasant surprise." Steadman's hand came down on Sparks's shoulder. "Thank you, Sparks. That will be all. We'll resume our discussion later."

"But"—Sparks shot his employer an impatient look—"we ain't got time."

"Nonsense. I've always got time for Clara. Do come in, my dear." He opened the door wide. "I'm sorry for the mess. I'm afraid you'll find us in a bit of disarray. I had to fire my housekeeper yesterday. Found the woman going through my personal papers." He led the way toward the parlor. They passed a room Clara had never seen into before. It must be his office. Steadman quickly closed the pocket doors on the chaos.

Clara glanced back toward the front door. Sparks loomed there, arms hanging down like a grizzly, his expression so loaded with animosity she couldn't resist stepping closer to Steadman.

"Come and sit down. Can I offer you some refreshment? As I said, I am without a housekeeper for the moment, but I can offer you at least some cool water after your long ride." Steadman seated her like a queen and took a chair himself, crossing his long legs and swinging one foot idly. "That garment is quite fetching, my dear."

Clara brushed aside his compliment. There was no time for flattery. "Steadman, I have something very important to tell you." She bit her lip. Her hands hurt, and she glanced down to see her fingers entwined tight, pressing red marks into each other. He'd be devastated to know he'd been duped by a man he trusted.

The door to the hallway stood agape. Where had Sparks gone?

She rose and hurried to the door, pushing it closed with a click. When she turned, she yelped in surprise. Steadman stood right behind her, and his hands reached for her. She hadn't heard him move at all.

"I'm sorry, my dear." He dropped his hands to his side. "I thought for a moment you were going to flee without telling me why you came. Please, sit down. I can see you're upset. Dare I hope your agitation is due to having arrived at an answer regarding my proposal?"

Instead of sitting, she walked to the window. Through the lace curtains, she had a view of the corrals and barn. Cattle dotted the hillside, grazing among the sagebrush and yucca. A lone cowhand carried a bucket from the trough toward the barn. Poor Steadman, were any of these cattle even his?

"You seem to have plenty of cattle." She pulled her gaze away from the corral to look at him.

Steadman had resumed his seat and recrossed his legs, relaxed, his eyes on her face. "Yes, Sparks assures me we must cull the herd to prevent overgrazing, especially in this hot weather."

Frustration at his gullibility strengthened Clara's resolve. "Steadman, listen to me. Sparks is a crook. The only reason your range is overrun with cattle is because he's been stealing them hand over fist. He's picked our ranch and the Double Box nearly clean, and he's using you to cover his tracks. Any cattle you've got to sell are rustled from area ranches."

Steadman went very still. For a long moment he said nothing. "That's a very serious accusation. Have you any evidence?"

"Yes. One of our hands, Trace McConnell, was shot yesterday. He was able to identify Sparks as the shooter. Sparks and your cowboys were driving a bunch of Cross B cows through Skull Canyon."

"I see." Steadman rose and went to stand by the fireplace. He clasped his hands behind his back and stared at the oil painting above the mantel. He held his body rigid. The poor man. He'd had such high hopes for his ranch, such big dreams, and now to be embroiled in a rustling ring, his own foreman using him like this. He must be humiliated, but they had to move quickly.

"We've got to ride to town and tell the sheriff. He'll come out here and arrest Sparks and his men." Clara crossed the room and put her hand on Steadman's shoulder.

He looked down at her, his expression bland. "My dear, surely you must know I can't show up at the sheriff's office with a story like this based solely on the testimony of a McConnell. They're jailbirds, and from what I gather, they have quite a history of menacing the town of Money Creek. I haven't liked to mention it before now, but I think your father is extremely unwise to keep those three on at the Cross B. He's being bilked right and left and doesn't even know it."

Clara stepped back, her hand dropping to her side. "You've got it wrong. My father isn't being bilked. You are. Look out your own window." She gestured toward the corral. "You're the only one who has cattle to sell. And they aren't your cows. And the McConnells are as honest as the day is long. They had a rather troublesome youth, but they're changed."

"I may be new to the territory, but I can read my own brand. Those are Lazy P cows, and Sparks says I haven't been as affected by the rustling because we're so isolated here on the backside of those Stovepipe Hills." He spoke slowly, as if to a child. His hands cupped her shoulders, and a small smile played across his lips. "No, my dear, if you're looking for rustlers, you should look no further than the Cross B bunkhouse. A McConnell is to blame for the missing cattle, not my foreman."

"How do you explain Trace getting shot?" Clara refused to believe him, no matter how logical and patient he tried to sound.

"Perhaps one of his fellow rustlers thought to take more than his share by bumping off one of his compatriots. I'm sorry. I know Trace was a friend of yours, and I'm sorry he's dead, but I can't say I'm sorry there is one less McConnell in your life. They're a bad influence on you. When we're married, you'll see the rightness of my words." He slid his hands down her arms and lifted her hands in his. "I do hope you've given my proposal serious consideration. I was sure when you came here today you were going to tell me you wished to be my bride." He brushed a kiss across her knuckles, his dark eyes penetrating hers with a challenge.

"Trace isn't dead." She withdrew her hands from his and resisted the urge to wipe them on her skirts. "The doctor says he's got a good chance of surviving. He'll tell Sheriff Powers about Sparks, and your foreman will be arrested. They hang rustlers in these parts. And you must have a care for yourself. As Sparks's employer, suspicion will be cast your way, too. Don't you see it? If you don't turn in Sparks yourself, people will think you were in on the stealing. You'll swing alongside your hired man."

The hallway door burst open, and Sparks strode in. "Devers, it's time to go. Get rid of the dolly-mop and saddle up."

Clara gasped. *Dolly-mop?*

"Shut up, Sparks."

She stepped back, shocked at the cold steel in Steadman's voice.

"You heard her. That fella I shot ain't dead. Sure as the sun's gonna come up tomorrow, he saw my face. We hafta ride. If you don't have the stomach to get rid of her, I'll do it." Sparks slid his gun from his holster and pointed it at Clara.

She dragged her stare away from the pistol to Steadman. The shock she expected to see wasn't there. His face had smoothed into hard lines. "You knew? You knew all along?"

"Put that away." Steadman rolled his eyes. "If you would use your brains instead of sitting on them all the time, you'd see we need her."

"What for?" Sparks lowered his gun, and Clara's breath returned.

"A hostage. Go saddle the horses. I'll get the money."

Sparks holstered his gun and left, slamming the front door behind him.

Clara moistened her lips and edged toward the door. If she could get to Hawkwing, she knew her horse could outrun any pursuer.

"Don't bother, my dear." Steadman reached into his coat and produced a gun. "Contrary to what you might have thought, I'm quite proficient with firearms." He'd returned to his haughty tone, but Clara wasn't fooled. This man, whom she had thought a greenhorn in need of assistance, was, under his silk-patterned waistcoat, a seasoned outlaw. He motioned her away from the door with the gun.

"Why are you doing this?"

He smiled. "Because I can. And it was such a sweet setup,

too. If Sparks hadn't been so careless, we'd have had our payoff soon. Do you have any idea how long this deal was in the making? The Boss has been laying the groundwork for more than two years. When he hears about this, he's going to—" Devers winced. "Well, let's just say it won't be pretty."

"Why do you need a hostage? Why not just let me go?" She stood in the center of the room, too far away to grab anything that might prove to be a useful weapon.

He winked at her, eyes glinting. "You don't know your own appeal, Clara. A little insurance wouldn't go amiss, I admit, but I anticipate other benefits of having you along." His leer made his intent unmistakable.

Anger and fear snarled in Clara's middle. She took one step toward the door, but his arm closed around her waist like a lasso, dragging her back. His other hand came up to squeeze her jaw, holding her head still. "Ah, ah, ah, we'll be leaving soon enough, my dear." His breath blew hot across Clara's cheek.

She clamped her hands on his arm and pushed, but she couldn't break his hold. She'd underestimated his speed and strength, just as she'd underestimated his involvement in the rustling. Knowing she was defeated for the moment, she allowed herself to relax.

"Much better." He stroked her cheek.

She wanted to spit in his eye but refrained. Better not to antagonize him. Her chance to escape would come.

He brushed a kiss across her temple. "You and I will settle our differences soon. For now, I think I hear Sparks with the horses." He grasped her elbow and headed toward the door, dragging her in his wake.

Sparks led two horses to the porch where Hawkwing waited.

"Tie her to the saddle, and I'll take her reins. I don't trust her."

Clara submitted to having her wrists wrapped in thin,

leather strips and fastened to her saddle horn.

Sparks spit a stream of brown juice that hit Hawkwing in the flank, making the horse shy and side-step. "Let's git." He lifted the reins and spurred his horse.

Clara cast a longing glance behind her toward the ranch road. But no help would come from there. Alec and Cal would be on the trail of Devers's crew deep in Skull Canyon. Alec probably didn't even know she was missing.

fifteen

Alec put his hand on Riley's neck and started up the slope with the dog. Heat pressed down on him, making him wish for a stiff breeze to cool his skin. Behind him, his men and Cal followed. Angus labored at the rear.

When they approached the top of the path, Alec hunkered down. Cal joined him, and together they inched forward onto their bellies, crawling to the edge to look down.

Perhaps two hundred cows milled in an open area. Cloven hooves churned the dirt. Riley wriggled close to Alec and lay down, putting his head on his forepaws, twitching his nose.

Two riders held the cattle below, forcing them along a post-and-rail fence that formed a V, channeling the animals toward a chute. Two more men operated the chute, enclosing one animal at a time. The odor of burnt hair and smoke grew stronger, as did the sound of bellowing from the animals below.

Cal nudged Alec's elbow and handed him a pair of field glasses. "Take a gander."

Every one of the cows on this side of the chute wore a bold Cross B on the right flank. The animals on the far side sported a fresh brand. He made out what appeared to be a Ladder 2. He'd never seen the brand before. Beyond the branding chute, the canyon widened out. More cattle than he could count spread out in a deep bowl of grass and scrub.

Alec had no idea the canyon was so wide here. And from the grazed-over look of the place, cattle had been held here for quite a while. His hands tightened on the glasses, making the magnified image before him shake with his fury.

Cal reached for the glasses again. "Beautiful plan. That Ladder 2 brand fits over the Cross B without any trouble at all." He kept his voice low. "Bet that's what happened to Seb's Double Box cows, too."

Alec nodded, not taking his eyes off the scene below. "They slip through the canyon, gather up some cattle, drive 'em here, change their brand, and sell 'em as soon as they have an order. Explains why nobody had any reports of Cross B or Double Box cows being sold. Pretty slick."

"Till you get caught. Bad for Trace that he stumbled across them in the act." Cal turned his glasses to the canyon rim.

Alec ran his hand across his rifle, his mind trying to formulate a plan. "You see Sparks?"

"Nope. Only the four down there. Don't see anybody watching from above."

Angus crept up and eased down on Alec's other side. Sweat ran from his temples. "What're you going to do?"

Alec rolled onto his hip and dug for his watch. He checked the angle of the sun and the face of his timepiece. "I think we ought to wait and give Powers time to come in from the east."

"Son, I don't think you should wait, especially for Sheriff Powers. We can take 'em. You, me, and Cal, we can each draw a bead on a man apiece from here. It'd take some tall shooting, but picking them off from up here would be the easiest way to keep from getting shot ourselves." Angus dragged his hand across his forehead and wiped the sweat on his shirt. "Those two boys you brought along are good cowboys, I don't doubt, but they've never been in a shootout before."

"All that drink has addled your brains. You couldn't hit the side of a barn with a scattergun if you were locked inside. Get back." Alec pointed down the slope behind him then turned to watch the action below.

Angus grunted then eased back. His movements scraped

on the scree-covered slope, causing a mini avalanche of pebbles to rain down.

Alec scowled. Might as well blow a bugle and announce their position.

"So we wait?" Cal passed him the glasses once more.

"We wait." Alec pulled off his hat and inched a bit closer to the rim. If Sparks wasn't here, where was he?

❧

Clara flexed her fingers, trying to loosen her bonds without drawing attention. Hawkwing sidled away from Devers's mount, not liking being dragged by his bridle.

Sparks pulled alongside and straightened her horse out. "I told Monty to finish up that last bunch of cows and drive the whole herd to the fort. He'll have them there in time to meet that army captain. Then he'll meet us at the rendezvous point with the gold." Sparks leaned over his horse's mane and spit a long, foul stream of brown tobacco juice into the brush.

Devers scowled across at his foreman. "This entire situation is your fault. I told you to go easy. I told you to take your time. But no, just like in La Junta. You have to get greedy and try to wipe everyone out in one go. We could've lived here for years, skimming a few head here and there. And now we're on the run again. I should've shot you a long time ago."

"Ha, you'd be nothing without me." Sparks shifted the wad in his mouth. "You'd be back at the poker tables trying to earn a living by fleecing cowpokes fresh off the trail."

Clara cast a glance back over her shoulder, trying to mark the way they'd come in case she found a way to get loose. Sparks and Devers had done nothing but bicker since leaving the ranch. The enormity and scale of their operation became evident the longer they argued. But they seemed not to care if she heard them. The thought froze her blood. She pulled harder at her restraints.

"Why'd we have to bring her along anyway?" Sparks jerked his thumb toward Clara. "She's slowing us down."

He'd broached the subject twice already, and each time Devers had told him to shut up. Devers ignored Sparks this time.

The trail narrowed up the side of the butte. They were forced to ride single file with Clara in the middle. She tried not to look down as they wound higher up the steep incline. Would anyone come for her? What if Alec was so angry with her he decided not to follow? She thrust that thought away as unworthy. Alec would come, no matter what she'd said to him. He was a man of honor.

"I think it's because you don't have the stomach to kill a woman." Sparks continued antagonizing Devers from behind Clara. "But you'll have to eventually. Or are you going to have me do it? I don't like killing a female, but it wouldn't be the first time." His laugh grated across Clara's skin. "She wouldn't even be the first Bainbridge woman I killed. Though it was Mrs. Bainbridge's own fault. She rode right in and found me setting up the dynamite charges to blow through the canyon. I had to kill her and make it look like an accident."

Blood swirled in Clara's ears, and she clutched the saddle horn and took great gasps to keep from fainting. Sparks had killed Mama?

"Shut your trap, Sparks. You talk more than an old woman." Devers shot a glare over his shoulder.

"What does it matter? She won't be telling anyone. And I figure she should know what happened before I kill her." Sparks spoke of murder as if talking about swatting flies. The man had no conscience.

Clara knew she wouldn't be able to call upon him for any clemency. As for Devers, he'd been as cold and remote as the mountains in the distance. Anger boiled inside her. She wanted to lash out, to hurt these men who had killed her mother, who had robbed her father, and who had caused her so much pain. Humiliation at being duped by Devers heated her blood and made her want to scream with rage.

No wonder he'd been so interested in the workings at the Cross B. Not because he wanted to learn about ranching, but because he wanted to know the best time to send riders to steal from the herd. She had played right into his hands, spilling information like a leaky bucket. And like an idiot, she'd allowed his flattery to sway her judgment and cloud her perception. All the times she'd defended Devers to Alec pierced her heart.

"Wish I'd brought some whiskey along. I could use a nip right about now." Sparks spit again.

Perspiration trickled down her back. Patches of white lather grew along the edge of the saddle as Hawkwing struggled up the trail.

They climbed for what seemed an eternity but was probably a couple of hours, with Sparks jabbering all the way, until they finally turned into a cut to their left. High, narrow walls pressed in.

The shade they provided cooled Clara. She had to duck under a jutting rock. When she straightened, they had emerged into a lush valley atop the butte they'd climbed.

Juniper ringed an open, grassy expanse. And at the far side, near a small, glassy pond, a log cabin huddled, dark and foreboding under the trees. Clara's heartbeat quickened. This must be the rendezvous point.

❧

Alec checked his watch again then nudged Cal with his elbow. "They're sure getting through those cows. Another hour or so and they'll be finished up here. Any sign of the sheriff?"

Cal trained his field glasses on the far end of the canyon.

"There's a lot of dust being kicked up down there. But I can't see anyone but the rustlers. How long are we going to wait anyway?"

Alec chafed under the inactivity. But the surest way to get someone killed or wounded would be to charge down there guns blazing. If one of the Cross B riders took a bullet because Alec was too impatient, he'd never forgive himself.

His men waited below. Younger than he, good cowboys, but not gunhands. Brave, loyal, and Alec's responsibility.

Movement in the trees to his left broke into his thoughts. A sick feeling washed over his chest. "Cal, where's Pa?"

Cal shrugged, still peering though the glasses. "Down with the boys, I guess. Hey, they stopped working. You think they're on to us?"

"That's why." Alec gritted his teeth and pointed.

Angus McConnell had emerged from the trees near the corral, his gun raised. "You boys throw down your weapons." Angus's voice sounded as scrawny as he looked.

"The idiot. He's blown the whole thing." Alec waved to his own men behind him, all the while kicking himself for allowing Angus to come along.

The rustler closest to Angus whirled his mount, grabbing for his sidearm. Angus let loose a blast from his own weapon that knocked him out of the saddle.

"That tore it." Cal shoved his field glasses aside and sighted down the barrel of his rifle.

The outlaw manning the gate raised his pistol and got off a shot at Angus before Cal winged him. Angus tottered, gripping his upper arm. His rifle clattered on the rocks as it fell from his hand.

"Pa!" The shout ripped from Alec's throat. He found himself skidding and sliding down the rocks toward his father. Cattle bawled and ran, tails up, eyes white-ringed. More shots rang out, but Alec couldn't tell who was doing the shooting. Riley passed him like a gray streak, heading into the cattle. Alec didn't have time to worry about his dog, not when his father might be dead.

Alec reached Angus, who lay sprawled in the open where he'd fallen. Blood ran from a deep gash in his upper arm. The cords in his neck stood out clearly as he gritted his teeth. Alec grabbed up both their rifles, then tucked his hand under Angus's good arm and dragged him back into the cover of the scrub trees. A glance above and behind told Alec that Cal and the Cross B cowboys were raining down lead on the rustlers.

"What were you thinking?" He dug his knife from his pocket and snapped open the blade. Two quick slashes and he'd gotten the sleeve cut away from the wound. "We were waiting for the sheriff."

Angus grunted. "A McConnell doesn't wait around for no sheriff, especially a back shooter like Powers. Those boys were fixin'—" He broke off when Alec used the torn sleeve to fashion a bandage, wrapping the wound tight to stop the flow of blood. Angus gasped, his narrow chest rising and falling in jerks. "Fixin' to pull out. I didn't want them to get away while we sat around waiting for Powers to show up."

A cow crashed through the trees near them making them both jump and dive for their rifles. Branches slapped off the animal's head and shoulders, and her bellow drowned out even the sound of gunfire. She swerved and disappeared into the pines.

Angus lay back. He let his rifle slide to the ground once more. "Rustler got off a lucky shot. Just winged me."

Anger built up like pressure in Alec's head. "You're lucky you're not dead. Of all the stupid things to do. I knew it was a mistake letting you come along. I knew I couldn't trust you.

I never could. You always find a way to screw things up. Now, stay here and keep your head down."

Alec crept to the edge of the trees. He forced himself to stop thinking about his father and concentrate on not getting killed. He used the milling cattle as cover to get closer to the branding pen.

One rustler lay on the ground, completely still. Another crouched behind a boulder on the far side of the clearing, firing up at Cal's location with his pistol. Blue smoke and tan dust hovered in the air. Where were the other two rustlers?

He reached the branding chute. A white-faced heifer bucked and thrashed, making splinters of the boards. The sound of her struggles masked any noise Alec's boots might have made as he eased closer to the outlaw behind the boulder. *Lord, don't let him turn around.*

Alec crossed the last ten yards of open space crouched over his rifle, ready to fire should the man turn. The gunfire from above ceased as Alec drew near. "Drop it." Alec pressed the barrel of his rifle against the back of the man's neck.

The rustler froze, his hands going up, the pistol dangling from his index finger by the trigger guard.

Rocks and pebbles tumbled off the slope. Cal, on his way down.

Alec reached out and took the handgun, tucking it into his belt. "Get up. Where's the rest of them? Where's Sparks?"

The rustler, a cowboy Alec had never seen before, lurched to his feet. Pale yellow whiskers dusted the man's cheeks. Eyes the color of straw narrowed to slits.

Cal approached, rifle held ready at his waist. "Alec, the other two got away. Where's Pa?"

Pa. All Alec's anger and frustration at his parent came rushing back in. He had to do something about Pa.

sixteen

A musty smell of old wood greeted Clara when Sparks shoved her inside the cabin. She squinted in the gloom, making out a stone fireplace, rough bunks along two walls, and a table that looked ready to collapse. Light came in around the wooden shutters on the window beside the door.

"Sparks, see to the horses. I'll see to our guest." Devers ducked to enter. His movement sent motes spiraling into the shaft of sunlight streaming in the doorway.

Clara grimaced, edging away from him on stiff legs. The way he said "our guest" made her want to retch. Her knee brushed against a chunk of log pushed up against the table, the makeshift chair polished from being sat upon so many times.

"I'm sorry the accommodations are crude, my dear, but outlaws can't be choosers, you know." Devers pulled off his gloves finger by finger, assessing her in a way that made her skin crawl. His insolent, possessive stare fired her anger.

"Drop the pretenses. You're no gentleman, so you can stop all the pretending. You're a worthless sneak thief with the ethics of a toad." Her hands fisted at her sides.

Devers laughed. "My, my, what a spitfire you are. I always suspected behind that pretty face a little rebel lurked." He smacked his palm with his gloves. "If you insist I drop the gentleman act, that's fine by me." He sneered at her. "Behaving like an outlaw suits me just fine." His gloves hit the table, and he stalked toward her, grabbing her upper arm and squeezing until tears stung her eyes. "It won't take me long to subdue you.

I'll break you like I would a temperamental filly."

His hot breath turned her blood cold. She trod on his foot with all her might and jerked her arm from his grasp. She swung her fist and connected with his chin.

He howled and hopped on one foot, his hand cupping his face.

Clara turned to run, but Sparks filled the doorway.

"Get her." Devers panted, eyes glaring.

Sparks grabbed her around the waist.

Clara kicked and thrashed, but she couldn't loosen his grip.

"Tie her up and toss her onto one of the bunks."

"I told you she'd be trouble. You give her half a chance, I bet she'd shoot you right between the eyes." Sparks grunted when one of Clara's heels connected with his shin. "I'll hold her while you get some rope off my saddle."

Clara found herself bound hand and foot, lying on the scratchy, straw-filled mattress of one of the lower bunks, her nose filled with the odor of musty cloth and a dozen unwashed riders who had lain in this bed before her. Her hair spilled across her face, but she couldn't reach up to brush it aside. Tears of frustration pricked her eyes, but she refused to give in to them.

"Lord," she whispered, "I know You can help me find a way out of this. But I don't want these bad men to get away. Please, somehow let Alec know how much I need him right now. And help me to be brave, to do what I have to do." She lay on her side, facing the room.

Devers rummaged in the wood box. Sparks leaned against the doorjamb, his rifle butt resting on his thigh, watching the narrow opening to this high, mountain canyon.

Clara shifted slightly, taking the weight off her hip but not wanting to draw any attention. The hard lump in her pocket quit biting into her side. She sent up another prayer, thanking the Lord for Alec and his gift to her. *And thank You, too, that no one thought to search me for a weapon.*

She'd have to wait until dark to fish it out and cut her bonds. But darkness was hours away. So much could happen before then.

⋙

Alec and his men rode toward Devers's ranch. Skull Canyon opened onto a high pasture dotted with more freshly branded Ladder 2 cattle. Just south of the ranch house, they met Deuce and the sheriff riding toward them. Behind the sheriff, a posse of half a dozen armed men followed, and in the midst of them, two riders looking very glum.

"We found these two racing toward town, so we thought we'd better grab them." Deuce grinned. "Guess you couldn't wait until I got there to start things?"

Alec motioned for Cal to bring up the rustler they'd captured. "There was another one, but he didn't make it." One of the Cross B riders led the horse with the body tied across it. "And we had one casualty."

Angus hunched in the saddle. His chin rested on his chest, and his eyes were closed. But his arm had quit bleeding. Though it must be hurting him, Angus hadn't complained.

Powers frowned. "You boys should've waited for the law to arrive. This looks very bad, you shooting one of Devers's riders without any proof." He leaned forward until his paunch hit his saddle horn. "If Devers wants to press charges, I'll have to lock you McConnells up until a trial can be arranged." His arrogant and familiar accusatory tone flicked Alec's strained patience.

"Proof?" Alec stood in his stirrups. He clenched the reins so hard, the leather bit into his palm and swung his arm wide. "The proof is back there in Skull Canyon. I don't have time for this." He turned to Deuce. "You passed by Devers's place on the way down here. Was there any sign of Sparks?

He wasn't in the canyon with these fellows."

"Nope, no sign of Sparks and no sign of Devers either. Kinda fishy, ain't it? Devers disappearing like that. He musta been in on it all along."

"You don't know that." Powers scowled.

Alec pulled his horse up next to the rustler they'd caught and grabbed the man by the collar. "Where's Sparks?"

The weedy-looking thief grinned, exposing bucked teeth in a nasty smile, but he said nothing.

Alec shoved him away. "Fine. One of your pards will talk. Deuce, bring those two other fellows over here."

"Now, just a minute," the sheriff protested, "I'm in charge here, and I'll question any suspects."

Though Powers blustered and tried to act tough when asking his questions, the three outlaws remained silent. Frustration mounted, for each moment they stalled gave Sparks more time to get away.

Alec finally had enough. "Deuce, you and the boys go back to the ranch and tell the Colonel what's happened. Me 'n Cal will go back to town with the sheriff and keep trying to crack these nuts. Maybe one of them will crawfish to save his own hide and tell us where Sparks and Devers might have gone."

They had barely parted ways when a rider on a fast horse approached from the north. Cal drew up. "That's the Colonel."

The horse skidded to a stop before them, lather coating his dark shoulders. The Colonel gasped, his hand trembling when he wiped his face. "Alec, Cal," he panted, "it's Clara. She's gone."

Worry slithered up Alec's spine, but he squelched it. "Clara and I had words this morning, and she took off on a ride to cool off. She'll be home soon."

The Colonel fought to catch his breath. "Trace asked for

her, and when I went to find her, her horse was missing from the barn. I left the cook to watch over Trace and followed her tracks. She went to Devers's place, but she's not there anymore. No one is, and the house looks like it's been ransacked. It looked like she left with two riders, heading this way, but I lost the trail." He sagged in the saddle as if he might topple to the ground at any moment. His hair seemed thinner and whiter than ever before, and his frame looked shrunken and stove in.

Dread slammed into Alec's chest. Clara, in the clutches of two desperate rustlers who had to know the lid had blown sky-high off their rustling racket? His mouth went dryer than a dustpan in the desert. Guilt followed hard on his despair. If he hadn't been such a callow brute, she never would've fled the house and gone running to Steadman Devers.

Urgent panic slammed through his chest. He had to find her. Rescue her, and tell her the truth. Tell her she was right about everything. "Colonel, we'll get her back."

"But how? We don't know where they went."

"I can find out." Alec dismounted and snapped his fingers. Riley bounded forward and stood before Alec, legs braced, eyes and ears alert. Alec reached up and dragged one of the rustlers out of the saddle and threw him to the ground. "Riley"—he pointed to the man—"guard."

The hair on the dog's neck rose, and his head lowered. His upper lips curled back to reveal his fangs, and a growl emerged from his throat that chilled even Alec. Riley scooted forward until his nose was bare inches from the wide-eyed rustler in the dirt. "Mister, I would suggest, for your sake, that you tell us where your boss went. Otherwise, I'm leaving you to the dog."

The prone man swallowed, never taking his eyes from Riley's snarling face.

"Hey now," one of the rustlers still in the saddle broke in.

"That's my brother. Call off your dog. I'll tell you what I know."

"Shut up, Lou." The thief mounted next to the sheriff struggled against the bonds tying his wrists. "Don't you tell them nothing."

"Stealing cattle is one thing. Kidnapping a girl is another, and I won't be no party to it." The one called Lou looked at Alec. "We was supposed to round up the rest of the cattle on the ranch and deliver them to an army major over by Silver City. Then we was supposed to bring the money to Devers at a cabin up in the hills southeast of here. Couple hours ride. Some place called the Lister Pass."

"Riley, sit." Alec called his dog off, patting the animal's head in approval.

Riley backed off and plopped his hindquarters into the dirt, tongue lolling, looking nothing like the fierce beast of a moment before, though he never took his eyes off the man in the dirt.

"Cal, you're with me. A couple hours means we'll get there near dark." Alec swung aboard his horse. "Colonel, we'll bring her home as soon as we can. Look after Trace, and"—he paused—"take my father back with you. He's got a gunshot wound that needs some tending. Get the doc for him, and I'll pay for it."

Angus's head came up, his eyes glowing with something Alec thought might be gratitude, though he'd never known Angus to be grateful for anything before. "No, son, I'm going with you."

Alec shook his head. "Forget it. You're hurt, and you're not up to the pace we'll be setting. Go with the Colonel, and I'll see you when I get back." Alec swung aboard Smoke and lifted the reins.

"Boy, when are you going to learn you don't own me and

you can't boss me? This is only a scratch. I've been hurt worse falling out of bed." Angus straightened in his saddle and stuck his chin out. "I'm going with you, and that's that. I've ridden that trail before. I can show you where Lister Pass is."

Like a horse on a short rope, everywhere Alec turned someone or something jerked his head around to a new direction. He needed to get to Clara quickly, and his father could help him do that, but his father also looked as if a toddler could knock him out of the saddle.

Guilt sat under his skin like burrs, pricking and pinching, but Alec shoved it aside and lifted the reins. "Let's get going then." He gave one long look at his father before turning in the saddle and legging Smoke into a trot. He whistled for Riley, who fell into a jog at his stirrup.

The buttes to the southeast rose up in a purple and yellow wall. Somewhere up there, two very bad men had Clara. *Please, God, forgive me for being such an arrogant fool and letting Clara fall right into their clutches. Forgive me for not telling the Colonel right away about the missing cattle so he could've been on his guard more. Forgive me for thinking I could handle all this on my own without asking for Your help.*

The Spirit prodded Alec's heart. *"How can you ask God for forgiveness when you know you've held a heart full of anger and bitterness toward another? 'Forgive us our debts as we forgive our debtors. If I regard iniquity in my heart, the Lord will not hear me. A broken and contrite heart, O God, you will not despise.'"*

Alec glanced over his shoulder to his father, who gripped the saddle horn with one hand and the reins with the other. Beads of sweat clung to his hairline. A dark, nearly black stain showed in the folds of the makeshift bandage. Another few inches to the right, and Angus McConnell would've breathed his last on this earth. And then what? Did he have a personal relationship with the Savior? Had Alec ever spoken to his father about spiritual things?

Alec swallowed the fist-sized lump in his throat. The answer was a resounding no. Everything Alec had learned and become since coming to the Cross B, everything the Bainbridges had taught him about God, about love and forgiveness, he'd only applied to himself, refusing to extend that forgiveness toward his pa. Instead, Alec had judged, scorned, and blamed Angus for all the ills and sins of the past. Alec had used Angus as an excuse to keep himself from expressing his true feelings to Clara, when the fault didn't lie with Angus but with Alec.

Alec wanted to shy from the truth. But he couldn't, not with the memory of Clara's angry, hurt eyes boring into him, not with God's Spirit whispering in his heart and shining a light on all the bad feelings he'd buried deep. Alec braced himself and allowed the truth to come forward.

Angus McConnell was no more or less guilty than Alec himself. Any sin was enough to separate a man from God. Though Alec could abhor the things his father had done— the abuse, the neglect, the lies—he could no longer harbor hate in his heart toward his father, not and expect the rest of his life to be right. Alec had been forgiven for his own sins, and obedience to God required he forgive Angus as well.

His chin drooped, and his breath rushed out. *Forgive me, Father. Forgive me for all the hate, the unforgiving heart, the hard feelings I've had toward Pa. Help me to remember that You love him just as much as You love me, that You sent Your Son for him, too. Help me to forgive him and love him like You do. I can't do this by myself.*

A weight slipped off Alec's shoulders as he confessed his sin. He raised his head and blinked hard.

Cal gave him a puzzled look.

Alec shook his head, not ready to put into words how light and clean he felt on the inside.

Alec slowed his mount until they had dropped back to where Angus rode. "You making out?"

Angus nodded.

Alec noted the dry, cracked lips and unwound his canteen strap from his saddle horn. "Here. You need this. You've lost a lot of blood." He found it hard, after all this time, to lay aside the old hurts, but he forced himself to say, "I'm glad you're with us. When this is all over, I think you and me need to have a talk. And I'll make sure the doc takes care of that wound."

Without giving his pa a chance to reply, Alec thrust the canteen into his hands and kicked Smoke into a canter. But he hadn't missed the gleam of hope that lit his pa's bloodshot eyes. Though Angus might never stop drinking, Alec knew he, himself, having shed that burden of unforgiveness, would never be the same.

seventeen

Tears streamed down Clara's cheeks. Her throat rasped, and she coughed. By turning her head on the mattress, she was able to tuck her nose and mouth toward her shoulder.

Gray smoke hung in the air like scarves. Devers flung the cabin door wide to allow the smoke to escape.

Sparks choked and held the crook of his arm over his face and swatted the air with his other hand. "What'd you want a fire for anyway?"

"I wanted some coffee." At Devers's words, a soft *whump* sounded, and a charred tangle of twigs and downy tufts fell from the stone chimney and extinguished the fire. "Stupid birds."

Clara took their moment of distraction and shifted on the bed until her hands lay near her hip. Slowly she inched her fingers into the folds of her skirt, stretching, searching. She almost cried aloud when she touched the smooth surface of her knife. Trying hard not to shake, she withdrew the pocketknife, closing her fist around it. Though darkness lay at least an hour away, she had a feeling time was running out for her.

Devers checked the sky then shot a glance at Clara. "When Hack gets here, we'll settle up, give him the boss's cut, and ride for California."

Hack? Where had Clara heard that name before? Devers closed the door again, throwing Clara into the shadows. She let out a shallow breath of relief and eased the knife open, trying to stifle the click of full extension.

"I wouldn't trust Hack any further than I could throw that

nasty pinto he rides. He's been skimming from the outfit for a long time. It's just nobody's been able to catch him with his hand in the poke." Sparks stared dolefully into the coffeepot then down at the bird's nest on the hearth.

Clara inserted the knife blade between her wrist and the ropes. She used tiny motions to saw at the ropes one strand at a time. Before she'd gone ten strokes, her wrist and hand began to ache from the awkward strain.

Devers sat on the upturned log and leaned back against the wall, propping his boots on the rickety table. "If I were you, I'd be thinking what I was going to tell the boss about why things blew up before he was ready to move. He's carved out a nice little life for himself in Money Creek. Things get too hot around here, he's going to have to pull up stakes, and he won't like that a bit."

Sparks scowled. "Wasn't all me. What do you think he's going to say when he finds out you took that girl?"

Clara froze. Hack. She swallowed hard. That was the man from the robbery stage who had put his filthy hands on her and threatened to take her. And here she lay trussed up like a field-dressed deer when he was on his way here.

Lord, help me. Help me find a way of escape. Does anyone even know I'm missing? Does anyone know where I am?

A cloud of peace that could only come from God wrapped around her. God knew where she was, and He could help her escape. She had her knife, and she had a little bit of time on her side before Hack appeared. She just had to use her head. Her aching fingers flexed around the knife, and she began to cut again.

The moment the bonds on her wrist broke free, someone outside shouted, startling Clara into dropping her knife. She gave a moan of dismay then bit her lip to quell any more noise.

Devers jumped to his feet and opened the door a crack.

Clara groped for her blade, wincing as her fingers closed around the sharp steel. The metal sliced her finger, but she was so glad to have the knife back in her hand, she barely felt the cut. Cold sweat broke out on her skin.

"It's Hack, and he's alone." Devers grimaced in the light from the open door. "Sure wish the boys had gotten here first. Hack won't like having to wait to get the money."

"Who does? The boys will be along. They had to drive the cattle to Silver City and get up here. They won't show up until after dark, I'm guessing." Sparks spit on the floor and hitched up his pants. He shifted from boot to boot and fingered the butt of the gun in his holster.

Devers opened the door, and Hack stepped inside. Short, rough, and every bit as mean as Clara remembered. She found herself inching back on the bunk away from his sweeping glare.

"Afternoon, Hack." Devers resumed his place at the table but kept his feet on the floor.

The runty outlaw put his fists on his hips. "How'd you two brainless sheep manage to foul up such a peach of a deal? The boss will skewer you boys when he catches up to you."

"Don't start with me. It was Sparks that blew it."

Sparks glowered at Devers's accusation but said nothing, keeping his attention on Hack.

"Never mind who blew it. The fact is it's blown, and the boss wants your livers for a snack. You got the money?"

"Not yet. Not all of it."

"Whaddaya mean, not all of it?" The outlaw's tiny eyes glittered.

Devers made tamping motions with his hands. "Don't worry. It should be here within the hour. My men are bringing it from the final sale of the stolen cattle."

"I don't have time to wait on your men." His small frame quivered with energy. "I want to be back on the trail before dark."

Clara must've moved or made a sound, because Hack spun on his boot to face her, his hand going for his gun. "Who's this?"

Clara gripped her hands together and lay still, too frightened to move. The black barrel of the six-shooter danced before her eyes.

"You don't need to worry about her." Devers rose from the table and edged toward Clara.

"Say"—Hack holstered his gun—"I remember her. She was on the stagecoach when you hit town." He licked his lips and rubbed his hands together. "Maybe I don't need to get right back on the trail after all. Maybe I have time for a little sport first." His footsteps scraped on the dirt floor, his mouth split in a leering grin.

"Now, hang on." Devers put his hand on Hack's arm. "That girl is mine."

Hack turned, his head moving like a snake's. "Don't mean I can't have a little fun with her. After all, I had to ride all this way, and you're making me wait on the money." He shrugged aside Devers's grip and turned again.

Clara pressed back against the cabin wall. She gripped the knife firmly, vowing to strike if he so much as touched her.

Sparks edged toward the door. "Reckon I'll keep watch." He edged out the door and closed it behind him.

"Stop, Hack." Devers interposed himself between Clara and Hack, his hands raised palms outward in a placating manner. His form blocked the weak light from the doorway and threw Clara into shadow again. "The girl is mine. I've been waiting for a long time to have her, and not you or Sparks, or even the boss himself is going to deny me. Not after all the work I put into this." His hand went to his gun, and he braced his legs apart.

His championship did nothing to belay Clara's fears. She scooted toward the foot of the bunk, wanting to be able to see all the men in order to evade them. With the rope still binding her ankles, she knew she'd have to take precious seconds to free herself.

Hack studied Devers for a moment then wiped his mouth with the back of his hand. "Fine. I wish you well with the spitfire. She's likely to put a knife in you at the first opportunity. You can see it in her eyes." He reached down and grabbed a handful of Clara's hair and gave it a yank. "A fiery one, no doubt. I'm not going to wait around here. I'll go back the way I came, circle around toward Silver City, and try to intercept the boys' trail. I can pick up the boss's money then and get it to him in town. You boys are on your own, but I'd suggest getting out of the territory quick. The boss will most likely figure you're too much of a liability to keep on. He's been known to cut his losses before."

Hack wrenched open the door, brushed past Sparks on the porch, and swung aboard his mount. Sparks entered the cabin again.

Clara lay frozen until the sound of hoofbeats faded away.

❧

"They were traveling pretty fast up this grade. Their horses must be played out." Alec surveyed the steep trail that wound up the side of the butte. "How much farther is it?" He turned to his pa, who sagged in the saddle.

"Couple of miles up then through a narrow cut of rock. The pass is like a bowl on top of this butte, steep walls, little pond, some trees. And a cabin. Used to belong to a prospector named Lister. Old-timer who used to come into town about once a year. Nobody knows what happened to him. He just quit coming in. But his cabin's still there. That'll be where those fellas have Clara. There's two ways into the pass. This one and another, rougher trail that heads the long way around toward Silver City." He closed his eyes as if his long speech had sapped the last of his strength.

A shiver of worry raced across Alec's skin. "How you holding up?"

"I'll make it. Don't fuss." A stubborn light, one Alec knew well from looking in the mirror, formed in Angus's eyes.

Cal looked quizzically at Alec. "What's gotten into you? Yesterday you wouldn't have cared if he fell right into Money Creek and drowned, and now you're fussing over him like a biddy with a new chick."

Alec shrugged, not knowing how to put into words all that God had been doing in his heart regarding his father. "Maybe I took a look inside and didn't like what I saw. Clara told me a few home truths, and Trace did, too. Made me realize all the harm I was doing to myself and those around me by hanging on to bitterness." He lifted his reins, uncomfortable baring his soul to his younger brother. "Let's push on."

Alec ignored Cal's bewildered look and glanced back to make sure Angus stayed close, then turned his eyes back to the tracks before him. *Lord, help me find her before anything bad happens to her. Keep her strong, and keep her safe.*

They climbed until they reached the narrow cut of rock denoting the entrance to the high meadow. "This is it. Go careful. They might have a lookout." Alec turned Smoke into the slot, ducking his head when the rocks closed in above to block out the light. Riley scooted through with plenty of room, his nose to the ground.

The instant Alec emerged into the open, he turned his horse sharply to the right and followed the rock wall until he reached the cover of a stand of junipers. Their scent wafted around him as he pushed through the branches and halted. His horse, gray as steam from a kettle, would stand out too much, even from a distance. Alec couldn't afford to alert the occupants of the cabin too soon. He snapped his fingers to Riley to stick close.

Cal dismounted when Alec did. Together they crept to the edge of the trees and scouted the terrain.

"Where's Pa?" Cal's whisper jolted Alec, making him realize he'd clenched every muscle.

"Isn't he behind you?" Alec peered through the branches toward the horses.

"He followed me into the cut, but he's not here now."

Frustration boiled along Alec's veins. "Maybe he fell back."

"Nope, look." Cal pointed off to their left. The tail of Angus McConnell's horse disappeared into the trees. "He's gone maverick again. Just like he did back in Skull Canyon with those rustlers. You think he plans to rush the cabin on his own?"

"He said there were two ways into this place. Maybe he's gone to make sure they don't get out the back door." Alec kicked himself for not thinking of it before.

Cal raised his field glasses and surveyed the scene.

"What do you see?"

"Only three horses. Hawkwing's one of them. They've been rode hard and put up wet. Sweat's dried on all of them. No smoke from the chimney, though I'd swear I could smell some. Must've lit a fire then put it out." He passed the glasses to Alec.

"Cabin looks like a good sneeze will flatten it. The door's open partway, but I can't see anyone moving inside."

"How do you want to play this? There's too much open ground around the cabin for us to get close without being seen. And we can't shoot at the place for fear of hitting

Clara." He glanced at the sky. "Be dark soon. That could be good or bad."

Riley must've caught Clara's scent, for his nose went up and his tail wagged. Alec put his hand on the dog's neck to quiet him.

Despair clawed up Alec's rib cage. *Lord, what do we do?* He took one more long look through the glasses then handed them back to Cal. "They took her for a bargaining chip, so let's bargain."

eighteen

"You told Hack where the boys were? You let him go get the money?" Sparks threw a pair of saddlebags against the wall. "Are you crazy? We're Jonahed for sure now. We'll never see a share of that money, you idiot. The boys won't have any reason to bring us our cut." His pistol cleared leather and pointed right at Clara. He cocked the gun, the chambers rotating ominously. "Ever since that girl entered the picture, you've been teched as a sky pilot. I've had it with the both of you."

Clara's heart hammered against her ribs, and she closed her eyes, not wanting to see him shoot.

"Devers, Sparks!" The shout from outside stopped Sparks.

Clara's eyes popped open. She knew that voice.

"This is Alec McConnell!"

Hope rushed through her. He'd come.

Sparks slammed the door shut with his boot and crouched beside the lone window. "What do you want?" Devers drew his gun and joined Sparks.

Clara moved quickly and slashed the rope binding her legs. There, now she was free. . .but only of the ropes. The distance to the door was too great to escape without one of the men gunning her down.

"I want the girl. Turn her loose, and you can go."

Devers shook his head and turned to Sparks. "No, I'm not giving up the girl."

"You're a fool, and so am I for letting you bring her in the first place. If we'd left her back there, they wouldn't have trailed us. I should shoot you right now," Sparks hissed through his teeth.

Clara inched to the edge of the bunk and put her feet on the floor. She swallowed hard, trying to keep her heart from beating so loud it would alert either of her captors.

"All we have to do is wait. Our riders will come. They're sure to outnumber McConnell and whoever he brought with him." Devers smiled, nodding, as if trying to get Sparks to believe him.

"You idiot. They won't come now. My guess is McConnell tumbled to what was going on in Skull Canyon and he took down the operation. There's no more money and no riders coming to help us. I say we give him what he wants. Let the girl go and make our escape." Sparks rose and turned to Clara. "Hey, what're you doing?"

Clara was edging toward the door.

Sparks stopped her in midstep. "She's loose!" Sparks moved to grab her, but a gunshot rang out. His face went slack in surprise, and he froze for a moment. Then his body melted toward the floor, landing outstretched before Clara, his hand flopping to the dirt at her hem. His rifle clattered to the ground. A red stain spread on Sparks's back.

She looked up, ears ringing from the shot.

Devers held his pistol at his waist, a faint wisp of blue smoke rising from the barrel.

Clara screamed and sprang for the door.

❧

Alec's heart hit his throat when the gunshot sounded then plummeted to his boots when Clara screamed.

Cal's arm thrust across Alec's chest to keep him from running toward the cabin.

The door burst open, and Clara emerged. But she only got as far as the porch steps before Devers clamped his arm about her waist. She struggled, kicking and pounding her fists against his grip.

Alec raised his rifle. "Hold it, Devers."

Devers pressed his gun against Clara's neck. She stiffened and went still. Devers's eyes flicked back and forth, looking for a means of escape.

Cal edged out of the trees, his gun trained on Devers, and stepped off to the left. Riley circled behind Alec, growling his displeasure, sensing Clara was in trouble.

"If you come any closer, I'll kill her." Devers cocked the pistol.

Alec's mouth went as dry as pillow ticking.

Clara's eyes pleaded with him to help her.

"Both of you, throw down your guns." Devers edged toward the corner of the cabin where the horses were tethered. "And keep that dog back."

"Let her go, Devers. If anything happens to her, I'll hunt you the rest of your days." Alec tightened his grip on his gun, knowing all hope was lost if he did as Devers said. "All we want is the girl. Let her go, and you can ride out of here."

"That's hardly likely, is it?" Devers changed the position of his gun until it pressed against Clara's temple and adjusted his hold on her, swerving to make sure she stayed between him and the guns trained on him.

Clara narrowed her eyes at Alec then looked at her hand.

A dull gleam caught his glance. *Ah, Clara.* The waning evening sun raced along the edge of a knife in her hand. He nodded ever so slightly that he understood. "This is your last chance, Devers. Let her go."

Devers laughed, his voice tinny with fear. He jerked Clara. "Untie the horses, and be quick about it." They edged between the mounts, blocking Alec and Cal from having a shot at him.

Alec's jaw tightened, and his hands grew slick with sweat. *Don't make a move, Clara, until I have a clean shot.* He willed the thought toward her, but she must not have caught it.

Instead of reaching for the reins to loose the horses from their tether, Clara reached up and back with her knife, slashing across Devers's unguarded ribs under his gun hand. At the same moment, she twisted and ducked, diving under Hawkwing's hooves and rolling out the other side.

Hawkwing snorted and threw up his head, further blocking Alec's line of fire. Riley raced past Alec like he was shot from a gun.

Devers screamed and clutched his side, then raised his pistol over Hawkwing's back toward Clara.

The dog skidded to a stop between Devers and Clara, legs braced, teeth bared.

Alec fired in desperation, but his shot went wide.

Another shot boomed from high up on the left. Devers rocked into the cabin wall and slumped to the ground. His pistol fell from his lax hand. The horses reared back, tearing away and scattering.

Alec ran to Clara and gathered her into his arms. As he held her tight, he looked up in the direction of the shot. The distinctive outline of Angus McConnell's battered hat showed on the rock rim.

Clara clung to Alec, shaking, taking deep breaths. The strength drained from him, and he sank to the ground with her in his embrace, stroking her hair and breathing a prayer of thanks. When Cal arrived, panting from his run across the clearing, Clara sprang out of Alec's arms and backed up until the cabin wall stopped her. Alec let her go, though he wanted to grab her up and pour out everything in his heart and head, to beg her forgiveness and plead for another chance. But she refused to even look at him. When she did manage to glance at his face, her eyes glistened with a trapped doe expression that made his heart ache. Best to give her some space to calm down.

Cal cleared his throat. "I'm sorry, Alec. I didn't have a clean shot at Devers." He bent to check on the dead man then straightened. "You all right, Clara? He didn't hurt you?"

She shook her head, her hair tumbling around her shoulders and a smudge decorating her cheek. Her body trembled as she stared at the knife still in her hand. She dropped it as if it burned her fingers. Riley whimpered and crowded close, licking her hand and wriggling against her leg.

Cal bent and retrieved the knife, wiped it on his thigh, then snapped it shut. He tossed it to Alec then entered the cabin. He came out again quickly. "Sparks is in there, shot in the back."

Angus eventually appeared, his hands clutching his rifle and looking as if a gesture might knock him over. "Son, I don't mean to hurry the lady, but I'd just as soon not be here if more of his friends are expected." He swiped his hand across his face and staggered.

Cal caught him. "Where'd you learn to shoot like that, anyway? Trace teach you?"

The old man straightened, a belligerent look in his eye. "*I'm* the one who taught *him*."

Alec shook his head. "Maybe we should wait until morning. You're done in, and so is Clara."

She lifted her head from his shoulder. "No, Alec, I want to go home. Please?" Those blue eyes melted his resolve.

Angus's idea that other members of Devers's gang could be on the way swayed Alec's decision. As dangerous as that trail would be in the growing dark, it would be worse to be pinned down here by outlaws. "All right. If you're sure. But we'll take it easy." There was so much he wanted to say to her, so much he needed to tell her, but her pallor and shakes told him now wasn't the time. He'd get her home and rested before he declared his feelings.

The ride seemed never to end. Cal rode close beside Angus, holding him in the saddle. The gunshot to his upper arm was worse than he'd let on, and they stopped twice to check the bandages and stanch the bleeding.

Clara remained silent and refused Alec's offer to put her in the saddle before him. She held out until they reached the road leading to the Cross B. As the moon gleamed down overhead, Alec lifted her from her horse and settled her before him. She leaned back against his chest and slept.

Alec let contentment seep through him. Surely now all would be well between them.

⤳

She avoided him for a week. The longest week of Alec's life. Figuring she needed time to recover from her ordeal, Alec waited, determined to be patient. But the longer he waited, the more his doubts grew. Maybe he should let well enough alone. Maybe he should forget about trying to bridge the chasm of awkwardness and hurt that yawned between them. Maybe he was a bucket-head for even thinking she'd ever forgive him. Whenever he entered a room, she was just leaving, and the one time he sent word to the house inviting her to come out with him for a ride, she'd refused. It appeared as if that door might be closed forever.

Angus rested in the bunkhouse, his arm stitched up by the fiery-headed doctor. Trace chafed under the same doctor's restrictions, but he, too, was on the mend.

Clara told them about Sparks's confession and the truth about Mrs. Bainbridge's death. The Colonel held her while she cried, and Alec kept his distance, knowing this was a sorrow father and daughter needed to share together.

Alec kept himself busy by rounding up the cattle in Skull Canyon and making an accurate count. When Judge Martin got the facts, his judgment was swift. The cattle were divided fairly between the Double Box and the Cross B, the court confiscated Devers's ranch, and the Colonel purchased it for the tax value of the land. Everyone was satisfied.

Except Alec. For weeks, ever since Clara's return home from Boston, he'd been avoiding her, and now that he wanted—no, needed—to see her, she avoided him. Despair that he had killed any love she felt for him pressed him lower and lower.

Perhaps he should consider leaving the Cross B. Once he had thought he could never leave this place, but now he found he couldn't stay, not loving Clara as much as he did and having her look right through him as if he wasn't there. Trace or Cal could take his place as foreman.

"Alec, the Colonel wants you up at the house. Said to meet him in the parlor." Trace leaned against the tack room door, pale, but obviously glad to be out of bed. "Sounded kind of urgent."

Alec put down the halter he'd been mending and squared his shoulders. Just as well. He could tell the Colonel of his decision to head west. His heart sat like a stone in his chest. How could something so busted up still be so heavy?

"I'll walk with you." Trace fell into step beside him all the way to the house.

&

"Clara, the Colonel sent me up to fetch you. He wants to see you in the parlor." Cal tapped on her open bedroom door. "Said to get you down there at a fast trot."

Clara turned from the window. Since the kidnapping, she'd done nothing at a fast trot. She moved as if weights hung from her limbs, caught in a lethargy and sadness she couldn't cast aside. Every harsh thing she'd said to Alec, every cruel accusation she'd flung at him, stung her like barbs. She'd judged him, condemned him, then threw at him her intention to marry another man—a man who turned out to be a thief, a liar, and a killer. And yet, because Alec was a man of honor, because of the debt he thought he owed the Bainbridge family, he'd come after her. She was so ashamed of herself, she couldn't even look at him, not wanting to see the hurt she'd caused, not wanting to see proof that she'd killed any hope of his loving her.

She entered the parlor with Cal on her heels. Before she was even three steps in, the doors closed behind her and the lock snicked fast. Puzzled, she turned around. "Cal?"

Alec strode in the opposite doors and stopped cold when he saw her. Over his shoulder, Trace slid the pocket doors shut. That lock clicked, too. "What is this?" Alec demanded.

Clara shrugged, bewildered. Her father was nowhere to be seen.

Cal's voice filtered through the door. "You two need some time to talk. Me'n Trace aren't letting you out of there until you fix whatever's broken between you."

"That's right." Trace's deep voice sounded from the other door. "If ever two people were meant for each other, it's you two. I know you said some hard things between you, but nothing that can't be forgiven, right, Alec? You've become a master at forgiving these days."

Clara took in Alec's stricken face and pounded on the door. "Calvin McConnell, open this door this instant."

"Nope, sort it out. And don't call me Calvin. I hate that." His boots scraped on the floor, and his footfalls faded along with his chuckling.

Clara turned to Alec, her hands spread. "Looks like we're stuck."

Alec nodded. "I'm sorry. I don't know what got into them." His mouth set a grim line. "Maybe it's just as well. I've been meaning to talk to you." Sadness lurked in his eyes.

Heat suffused her cheeks, and she dropped her chin. Her tongue stuck to the roof of her mouth, cutting off anything she might say, all the apologies she needed to utter. Shame stopped her voice.

"I'm real glad you're home safe. I prayed like crazy for you the whole time Devers had you."

She nodded her thanks, still unable to look him in the eye. Then his boots came into view. How had he crossed the room so quickly and quietly?

He took her chin in his fingers and forced her face up. "Clara, why won't you talk to me? I've been waiting for you to be yourself again. There's so much I need to tell you."

The tenderness and uncertainty in his eyes speared her. "Alec, I. . ."

He sucked in a deep breath, his chest rising. "I wanted to tell you how right you were, all those things you said to me. I had to take a good hard look at myself, and I didn't like what I saw. I'm sorry, Clara."

She inhaled the scents of leather and sunshine and hay that always surrounded him. She'd wronged him, and here he was, apologizing to her. "No, Alec," she forced the words past the knot of guilt in her throat. "I was wrong to accuse you so. I was hurt and angry and scared. I had no right to judge you so unfairly."

A smile teased his lips. "I can't say your words didn't hurt, but sometimes the truth does hurt. You said what I needed to hear in the only way I would understand. I'm not sure what scared me more, the thought of how ugly I'd become on the inside or the thought of losing you to Steadman Devers." His thumb traced her jawline sending shivers across her shoulders and down her arms.

"No, that's not true. I know which one scared me more. Clara, I'm a changed man because you told me the truth. I wanted you to know before I left that I'll never be the same again. And I'll love you till my last breath." His hand fell away, leaving her chilled and feeling the loss.

He was leaving? "You're leaving?" The words came out a strangled choke.

He stepped back and tucked his thumbs into his back pockets and studied the rug. "Yeah, it's time for me to move on. I can't stay here, seeing you every day, loving you like I do but not being loved in return. I know I killed those feelings through being a hardheaded ignoramus, so I don't blame you at all, but I just couldn't take it staying here."

Clara blinked. "You think I don't love you? Where'd you get an idea like that?"

His head came up, a hopeful light flashing in his brown eyes. But his expression remained wary, as if he couldn't dare to believe her. "Well, you were all set to marry another man."

Her hands flew out and up. "Oh, Alec, I never meant that. I was just so frustrated and angry with you. I guess I wanted to hurt you like you'd hurt me. But I was wrong."

She had to convince him, but how? In an instant she knew.

Clara stepped close and boldly raised her arms about his neck. Her fingers tunneled into the unruly brown hair at the nape of his neck. "Alec McConnell, I'll love you until the day I die. I think I've loved you since the moment I saw you, all defiant and scared in that jail cell. Say you forgive me, and say you'll stay."

His arms came around her and crushed her to him. She lifted her lips to his kiss, not caring that the salt of her tears mingled with the sweetness.

He broke the kiss to whisper against her temple. "Ah, Clara, do you know how long I've wanted to hold you in my arms and hear you say you love me? And how long I've wanted to say I love you in return?" His warm breath feathered against her skin, heating it and sending chills up her spine all at once.

"And you forgive me?" She leaned back in his arms to stare up into his beautiful brown eyes.

"Forgiveness is something I'm getting better at all the time." He kissed her once again.

A muffled cough sounded outside the door. "Think we can let them out now?" Trace's solemn question trickled toward them.

"Maybe. It's awful quiet in there. They've either made up, or they've killed each other." Cal chuckled. "Which do you think it is?"

Alec squeezed her tight, the lines of worry gone from his expression. "All right, you polecats. You've made your point. Unlock the door and vamoose."

"Clara?"

"Yes, Cal?" She didn't take her eyes from Alec's as she raised her voice toward the door.

"Everything worked out to your satisfaction?"

"Yep." Laughter bubbled up.

"Alec?" Cal persisted.

"What?"

"You been roped and branded by that little gal?"

"Happily."

" 'Bout time."

The lock clicked and boots clomped away down the hallway. The front door banged.

Clara reached up and cupped Alec's cheeks in her palms. Though she knew every feature by heart, she drank in his eyes and hair and lips. Being in his embrace, knowing she was loved and could express her love for him, was better than she'd dreamed. "You're mine now, cowboy."

"I've always been yours, Clara, heart and soul."

A Letter To Our Readers

Dear Reader:

In order that we might better contribute to your reading enjoyment, we would appreciate your taking a few minutes to respond to the following questions. We welcome your comments and read each form and letter we receive. When completed, please return to the following:

Fiction Editor
Heartsong Presents
PO Box 719
Uhrichsville, Ohio 44683

1. Did you enjoy reading *Clara and the Cowboy* by Erica Vetsch?
   ❏ Very much! I would like to see more books by this author!
   ❏ Moderately. I would have enjoyed it more if

   _____

   _____

   _____

2. Are you a member of **Heartsong Presents**? ❏ Yes ❏ No
   If no, where did you purchase this book? _____

   _____

3. How would you rate, on a scale from 1 (poor) to 5 (superior), the cover design? _____

4. On a scale from 1 (poor) to 10 (superior), please rate the following elements.

   ____ Heroine   ____ Plot
   ____ Hero   ____ Inspirational theme
   ____ Setting   ____ Secondary characters

5. These characters were special because? _____

_____

_____

6. How has this book inspired your life? _____

_____

_____

7. What settings would you like to see covered in future
   Heartsong Presents books? _____

_____

_____

8. What are some inspirational themes you would like to see
   treated in future books? _____

_____

_____

9. Would you be interested in reading other **Heartsong
   Presents** titles? ❏ Yes ❏ No

10. Please check your age range:
       ❏ Under 18   ❏ 18-24
       ❏ 25-34   ❏ 35-45
       ❏ 46-55   ❏ Over 55

Name _____

Occupation _____

Address _____

City, State, Zip_____

E-mail _____

The
Anonymous
Bride

Sometimes the one you love is right before your eyes.

Historical, paperback, 352 pages, 5.5" x 8.375"

Please send me ____ copies of *The Anonymous Bride*. I am enclosing $12.99 for each.
(Please add $4.00 to cover postage and handling per order. OH add 7% tax.
If outside the U.S. please call 740-922-7280 for shipping charges.)

Name _____

Address _____

City, State, Zip _____

To place a credit card order, call 1-740-922-7280.
Send to: Heartsong Presents Readers' Service, PO Box 721, Uhrichsville, OH 44683

Hearts♥ng

HEARTSONG PRESENTS TITLES AVAILABLE NOW:

Presents

___HP799 *Sandhill Dreams*, C. C. Putman
___HP800 *Return to Love*, S. P. Davis
___HP803 *Quills and Promises*, A. Miller
___HP804 *Reckless Rogue*, M. Davis
___HP807 *The Greatest Find*, P. W. Dooly
___HP808 *The Long Road Home*, R. Druten
___HP811 *A New Joy*, S.P. Davis
___HP812 *Everlasting Promise*, R.K. Cecil
___HP815 *A Treasure Regained*, P. Griffin
___HP816 *Wild at Heart*, V. McDonough
___HP819 *Captive Dreams*, C. C. Putman
___HP820 *Carousel Dreams*, P. W. Dooly
___HP823 *Deceptive Promises*, A. Miller
___HP824 *Alias, Mary Smith*, R. Druten
___HP827 *Abiding Peace*, S. P. Davis
___HP828 *A Season for Grace*, T. Bateman
___HP831 *Outlaw Heart*, V. McDonough
___HP832 *Charity's Heart*, R. K. Cecil
___HP835 *A Treasure Revealed*, P. Griffin
___HP836 *A Love for Keeps*, J. L. Barton
___HP839 *Out of the Ashes*, R. Druten
___HP840 *The Petticoat Doctor*, P. W. Dooly
___HP843 *Copper and Candles*, A. Stockton
___HP844 *Aloha Love*, Y. Lehman
___HP847 *A Girl Like That*, F. Devine
___HP848 *Remembrance*, J. Spaeth
___HP851 *Straight for the Heart*, V. McDonough

___HP852 *A Love All Her Own*, J. L. Barton
___HP855 *Beacon of Love*, D. Franklin
___HP856 *A Promise Kept*, C. C. Putman
___HP859 *The Master's Match*, T. H. Murray
___HP860 *Under the Tulip Poplar*, D. Ashley & A. McCarver
___HP863 *All that Glitters*, L. Sowell
___HP864 *Picture Bride*, Y. Lehman
___HP867 *Hearts and Harvest*, A. Stockton
___HP868 *A Love to Cherish*, J. L. Barton
___HP871 *Once a Thief*, F. Devine
___HP872 *Kind-Hearted Woman*, J. Spaeth
___HP875 *The Bartered Bride*, E. Vetsch
___HP876 *A Promise Born*, C. C. Putman
___HP877 *A Still, Small Voice*, K. O'Brien
___HP878 *Opie's Challenge*, T. Fowler
___HP879 *A Bouquet for Iris*, D. Ashley & A. McCarver
___HP880 *The Glassblower*, L.A. Eakes
___HP883 *Patterns and Progress*, A. Stockton
___HP884 *Love From Ashes*, Y. Lehman
___HP887 *The Marriage Masquerade*, E. Vetsch
___HP888 *In Search of a Memory*, P. Griffin
___HP891 *Sugar and Spice*, F. Devine
___HP892 *The Mockingbird's Call*, D. Ashley and A. McCarver
___HP895 *The Ice Carnival*, J. Spaeth
___HP896 *A Promise Forged*, C.C. Putman

Great Inspirational Romance at a Great Price!

Heartsong Presents books are inspirational romances in contemporary and historical settings, designed to give you an enjoyable, spirit-lifting reading experience. You can choose wonderfully written titles from some of today's best authors like Wanda E. Brunstetter, Mary Connealy, Susan Page Davis, Cathy Marie Hake, Joyce Livingston, and many others.

When ordering quantities less than twelve, above titles are $2.97 each.
Not all titles may be available at time of order.

HEARTSONG
PRESENTS

If you love Christian romance...

$10.⁹⁹

You'll love Heartsong Presents' inspiring and faith-filled romances by today's very best Christian authors...Wanda E. Brunstetter, Mary Connealy, Susan Page Davis, Cathy Marie Hake, and Joyce Livingston, to mention a few!

When you join Heartsong Presents, you'll enjoy four brand-new, mass-market, 176-page books—two contemporary and two historical—that will build you up in your faith when you discover God's role in every relationship you read about!

Imagine...four new romances every four weeks—with men and women like you who long to meet the one God has chosen as the love of their lives...all for the low price of $10.99 postpaid.

Mass Market 176 Pages

To join, simply visit www.heartsong presents.com or complete the coupon below and mail it to the address provided.

✂- -

YES! Sign me up for Heartsong!

NEW MEMBERSHIPS WILL BE SHIPPED IMMEDIATELY!
Send no money now. We'll bill you only $10.99 postpaid with your first shipment of four books. Or for faster action, call 1-740-922-7280.

NAME _____

ADDRESS_____

CITY_____ STATE _____ ZIP _____

MAIL TO: HEARTSONG PRESENTS, P.O. Box 721, Uhrichsville, Ohio 44683
or sign up at WWW.HEARTSONGPRESENTS.COM